Manners and Mischief

A Samantha Classic
Volume 1

by Susan S. Adler *and* Maxine Rose Schur

American Girl®

Published by American Girl Publishing

Questions or comments? Call 1-800-845-0005, visit **americangirl.com**, or write to Customer Service, American Girl, 8400 Fairway Place, Middleton, WI 53562.

Printed in China
14 15 16 17 18 19 20 LEO 11 10 9 8 7 6 5 4 3

Cover image by Michael Dwornik and Juliana Kolesova

Cataloging-in-Publication Data available from the Library of Congress

To my parents,
who made childhood beautiful,
and to David, Rachel and Daniel,
who keep childhood open to me
—S.A.

To Liliana, Cecilia,
and Susana
—M.R.S.

Beforever™

The adventurous characters you'll meet in
the BeForever books will spark your curiosity
about the past, inspire you to find your voice
in the present, and excite you about your future.
You'll make friends with these girls as you share
their fun and their challenges. Like you, they are
bright and brave, imaginative and energetic,
creative and kind. Just as you are, they are
discovering what really matters: Helping others.
Being a true friend. Protecting the earth.
Standing up for what's right. Read their stories,
explore their worlds, join their adventures.
Your friendship with them will BeForever.

TABLE *of* CONTENTS

Jessie

CHAPTER 1

Samantha!"

The voice broke through the summer afternoon like a crack. The leaves of the quiet old oak tree suddenly rustled and dropped a squirming bundle of arms and legs. Samantha Parkington tumbled out of the tree.

"Samantha, you're really dumb," the voice continued. It was coming from a hole in the hedge that separated Samantha's house from Eddie Ryland's. "You're so dumb, you don't even know how to climb a tree."

Samantha glanced at her scraped and bleeding knee and looked pained—not because of the knee, but because the voice was at it again. She glared at its owner with a look that could have frozen water in July. "Go away, Eddie."

But Eddie's round, sticky face didn't go away. "You're so dumb, you probably think three times four is twelve," he said.

"Eddie." Samantha looked disgusted. "Three times four *is* twelve."

"Well, anyway, you're so dumb—"

That was enough for Samantha. "Eddie," she said, "if you don't get out of here right now, I will take your entire beetle collection from behind the shed, and I'll put it in the offering plate at church on Sunday." She paused to be sure he was listening. "And I'll tell your mother *you* did it."

Eddie's eyes grew wide. He pulled his mouth into a frog face and left to find a safer hiding place for his beetle collection.

Samantha examined her knee. The bleeding had stopped, but her stocking was badly torn. She could picture how Grandmary would look when she saw it. Grandmary's eyes had a soft, warm light when they looked at Samantha, but her face could be very stern when she talked about growing up. "Discipline," Grandmary always said, "is what turns girls into ladies."

Samantha tugged at the hole in her stocking, but she couldn't hide it. The taffeta bow that had held her dark brown hair drooped over her forehead. Yes, this was a job for Jessie.

Samantha hurried up the walk and climbed the porch steps two at a time. At the front door, she slowed down. If there was any noise at the front door, Elsa might come. Elsa was the new maid. She was always grumpy, and Samantha didn't want to listen to a lecture now.

Luckily, the door was quiet. No one saw Samantha run all the way to the third floor. There, at the end of the hall, was the sewing room. And in the corner sat Jessie. She had fine brown skin, dark eyes, and a wide, bright smile. Yards and yards of soft pink material tumbled around her, and the sewing machine clicked quietly as her feet pressed the treadle back and forth. She hummed to its rhythm as her delicate hands guided the cloth past the flashing needle.

Jessie made clothes for the household. She was working on a new dress for Grandmary, but she stopped as Samantha came through the door.

"Oh, Miss Samantha, just look at you," Jessie said.

As she stood and turned, Jessie's large floating apron swirled over the baskets of thread and laces that rested on the floor. "What have you been up to? No, don't tell me. I don't want to know. Here you are, nine years old, almost a lady, and still getting into mischief like a ragamuffin. What will your Grandmary say?"

Samantha folded her hands and looked at the floor until Jessie was quiet. The mild scolding was a small price to pay for the help she knew Jessie would give her. Already Jessie had brushed the grass and dust from her hair. Now she checked Samantha's dress for tears and stains. She spotted the torn stocking.

"Take off those shoes and stockings right now. Does your knee hurt?" asked Jessie.

"No, Jessie, it's all right. I'd just rather not have to explain to Grandmary," said Samantha.

Jessie smiled and reached for her sewing basket. Samantha found a small clean rag and wet it from the water pitcher. She sponged her injured knee while Jessie sat down to repair the damaged stocking.

As Samantha looked around the room, she noticed a piece of jelly biscuit on the floor. She must have dropped it the day before. Three ants had found it. She was about to tell Jessie when she noticed two more ants on their way. It would be fun to see how many would come.

Samantha sighed loudly. "It must be awfully boring to be grown up," she said.

Jessie laughed softly. "Well, that depends. It depends a lot on the person. Now you, Miss Samantha, I don't think you'll have to be worried about being bored, even when you're grown up."

There were seven ants on the jelly biscuit now.

"I'll bet Cornelia isn't bored," said Samantha.

Jessie laughed again. "No, I don't imagine Miss Cornelia is very often bored," she said. Cornelia was a friend of Samantha's favorite uncle. She was pretty and dark haired, and she laughed easily. Anyone could see that she liked Uncle Gard a lot. But Samantha didn't think Cornelia was right for Uncle Gard. She thought someone like Alice Roosevelt, the President's daughter, would be better. Alice Roosevelt did the most exciting things, and the newspapers were always talking about her.

"Is Uncle Gard going to marry Cornelia?" asked Samantha.

"That's none of our business," Jessie said firmly. "And children shouldn't ask such questions."

Samantha grumbled softly. "A minute ago I was almost a lady. Now I'm a child again."

Twelve ants were on the biscuit, and three were on the way.

"Uncle Gard is a spy, you know," Samantha said.

"Miss Samantha!" Jessie's head shot up in surprise. "Where do you get such foolish ideas?"

"Well, he *should* be a spy," Samantha went on. "He's so handsome and brave, everyone would just fall in love with him. He could get their secrets, and they'd be so in love with him, they wouldn't even care."

"I think you'd better keep such ideas to yourself," Jessie said as she looked closely at the hole she was mending. "You've made quite enough trouble for one day."

There were nineteen ants around the jelly biscuit.

"Jessie, did you know my mother and father?" Samantha asked.

Jessie spoke gently. "You know I didn't, child. That accident in the boat happened when you were just five. You know I didn't come to work for your grandmother till you were seven."

Samantha had known that. Asking had really been wishing. She touched the locket pinned to her dress. Inside the small gold heart was a picture of her mother and father. She would have loved to hear Jessie talk about them. When Jessie told stories, she made everything sound like magic. Jessie would have made Samantha's parents seem like a prince and princess.

"Tell me about New Orleans, Jessie. Please?"

Jessie picked up a piece of silk for the sleeve of Grandmary's new dress. Her musical voice began to tell about a place where flowers bloomed in winter, a place where there were huge white mansions and balconies made of iron that looked like lace. She told about spicy shrimp and about music and dancing in the streets. And the best part was, everything Jessie said was true. She didn't have to make up stories about faraway places. Her husband, Lincoln, was a porter on the train that ran to New Orleans. Lincoln brought home wonderful tales of the places he'd seen and the people he'd met. And he never forgot Samantha. She had a scrapbook almost full of colorful postcards that he sent her from all of his trips. Sometimes he brought her pralines from New Orleans—brown sugary candy crowded with sweet pecans. Jessie and Lincoln made Samantha's world wide and wonderful. An hour passed easily with Jessie's soft voice carrying Samantha to dreamlike places.

A New Girl

CHAPTER 2

t four o'clock, Samantha stood outside the parlor doors, looking like new. It was time for her hour with Grandmary. Samantha's hair was combed, her ribbon was perfect, her skirt hung straight, and her stockings were repaired. She knocked softly on the door, then slipped through and made a quick curtsy to her grandmother.

Samantha thought Grandmary looked like a queen, especially during their sewing hour. Grandmary sat up very straight. Her velvet chair looked like a throne with her silk gown flowing around it. Her white hair seemed made for a crown, with never a strand out of place.

Samantha always *tried* to be a young lady, but it was a lot easier to remember how when Grandmary was watching. Samantha noticed that everyone behaved more like a lady when Grandmary was around.

"Good afternoon, Samantha," said Grandmary.

"Good afternoon, Grandmary." Samantha squirmed ever so slightly. She didn't know how, but Grandmary always seemed to know when she had been into mischief. But today Grandmary didn't ask questions. Instead, she smiled.

"Sit down, my dear," Grandmary said. She handed a basket to Samantha. "You must try to work a little harder on your sampler. It's not going very quickly."

"Yes, Grandmary." Samantha took her seat on a chair next to her grandmother. She picked up her sampler and sighed a little. When it was finished, the sampler would read "ACTIONS SPEAK LOUDER THAN WORDS." Grandmary had explained this saying. She said it meant that how people act is more important than what they say. Samantha tried to imagine the words sewn in pink silk thread. Around them would be flowers and fruits made of complicated stitches that would show off her sewing skills. But the skills were slow in coming. So far the sampler read "ACTIONS SP."

Samantha stuck her tongue between her lips as she concentrated on a hard stitch. She glanced sideways to see if her grandmother looked in a good mood.

"Grandmary," Samantha began.

"Yes, dear?"

"Did you see the doll in Schofield's shop?" Samantha asked.

"Yes, dear, I did," answered Grandmary.

"Isn't she beautiful?" sighed Samantha.

"It's quite a nice doll," Grandmary said.

"Do you think I might have her?"

"Samantha, that is an expensive doll," said Grandmary. "It costs six dollars. If you are going to grow up to be a responsible young lady, you must understand the value of a dollar."

"I could earn the money to buy her, Grandmary. I could make boomerangs and sell them. *The Boys' Handy Book* shows just how to do it. I could—"

"Samantha!" Grandmary was shocked. "A *lady* does not earn money."

Samantha had known there wasn't much hope, but she added very quietly, "Cornelia says a woman should be able to earn money. She says women shouldn't have to depend on men for everything. She says—"

"Cornelia has a great many newfangled notions," announced Grandmary. "She should keep them to herself."

Samantha turned back to her work with a sigh. "I would have called the doll Lydia," she said softly. "She looks like my mother."

Grandmary was startled. Then her eyes softened. A moment later she said, "There are other ways, my dear, to reach your goals."

Samantha looked up hopefully. Grandmary continued, "If you do well at your tasks, you might earn the doll. If you practice your piano daily—"

"Oh, Grandmary, I will." Samantha was delighted. "I'll practice an hour every day. I'll make my sampler beautiful. I'll help Mrs. Hawkins. I won't get my dress muddy. I—" She was about to say she wouldn't tease Eddie Ryland, but she knew there were some promises she just couldn't keep. "Oh, Grandmary, thank you!" Samantha threw her arms around her grandmother.

"There, there, my dear. We shall see," said Grandmary with a slight note of caution in her voice. "We shall see how you do."

Samantha worked hard on her sampler for half an hour. Then, from down the street, she heard a low rumble. Soon there were great pops and bangs. As the noise grew louder, angry voices and the frightened whinnies of horses joined it. Samantha jumped up from her seat and ran to the window.

"Oh, Grandmary, it's Uncle Gard. It's Uncle Gard and Cornelia!" Samantha called.

Grandmary raised her eyes to the ceiling. "He's brought that dreadful automobile again. Whatever shall I tell the neighbors!"

Samantha could hardly contain her excitement as the shiny black car jerked and sputtered to a stop in front of the house. Two people climbed out. They wore long coats that covered them from head to toe. Cornelia wore a hat tied down with a scarf, and Uncle Gard wore large goggles that made him look like an overgrown fly. They came up the walk laughing and beating the dust from their hats and coats.

The bell rang. A minute later, Hawkins appeared at the parlor door looking dignified. It seemed to Samantha that the more confusion there was, the more dignified Hawkins became. "Mister Gardner and Miss Cornelia, Madam," he said.

"Very well, Hawkins. Show them in. And tell Elsa to bring tea," said Grandmary.

The couple burst into the room, bringing laughter and the smell of summer with them. "How are you, Mother? You look wonderful," said Uncle Gard. He gave Grandmary a big hug, and she couldn't help smiling.

"Good afternoon, Gardner. Good afternoon, Cornelia," said Grandmary. "I am fine, thank you, Gardner. But I was a good deal better before you shattered the peace of the entire neighborhood with that horrible machine of yours. Why must you bring it here?"

Uncle Gard's eyes were laughing. "Now, Mother, this is 1904. You've got to keep up with the times. Besides," he winked at Samantha, "how can I teach Sam to drive if I don't bring the automobile?"

"Oh, Uncle Gard, will you really? Will you?" Samantha was popping with excitement.

"Sure I will. Come on. I'll take you for a ride right now."

"Indeed, you won't," said Grandmary. "What can

you be thinking of? Why, her clothes would be ruined!"

Samantha's face fell.

Cornelia looked at her quickly and said, "It's all right. She can wear my duster. It's a little too big, but we'll make it fit, won't we, Samantha?"

As they walked into the hall to fix the coat, Samantha gave Cornelia a grateful smile. Minutes later, she headed down the walk, trailing the hem of the long coat behind her.

Eddie Ryland had been sitting in the car, but he scampered down as Samantha and her uncle approached.

Uncle Gard lifted Samantha up to the seat. "Hold tight, Sam, while I crank it up," he said.

"You sure look dumb, Samantha," Eddie teased. He never stopped.

Samantha wasn't listening. She held tight as Uncle Gard cranked and the car began to lurch.

"Anyway, I know something you don't know," Eddie said loudly so that Samantha could hear him as the car rumbled.

Uncle Gard jumped into the seat next to Samantha and took hold of the steering wheel. The car began to bounce and sway into the middle of the road.

"A girl's coming to live at our house. She's nine, just like you," Eddie hollered over the noise.

"You're lying, Eddie Ryland!" Samantha yelled and choked on the dust.

"I am not! Her name's Nellie!"

Samantha didn't even try to answer. She was holding on for dear life as that most modern of inventions, the automobile, bucked and rumbled its way toward town.

Back at the front door, Grandmary shook her head. Just as she turned back to the parlor to join Cornelia for a cup of tea, she saw Jessie scurrying from the kitchen. There was something in her hand.

"Jessie, what's the matter?" asked Grandmary.

As Jessie hurried up the stairs, she called over her shoulder, "It's pepper for the sewing room, ma'am. There are ants up there. Hundreds and hundreds of ants!"

The Tunnel

CHAPTER 3

everal days later, Samantha bounded into her backyard holding a gingerbread cookie. She had just finished practicing the piano. She practiced piano every day now, for one whole hour. That hour certainly did seem long. She couldn't wait to get outside when it was over.

Samantha took a deep breath of summer air and a couple of long leaps. She stopped beside the tunnel.

The tunnel was a hole worn in the lilac hedge between her house and the Rylands', but Samantha had always called it "the tunnel." Through it now, she could see a girl. The girl was busy hanging laundry in the Rylands' yard. Could Eddie possibly have been telling the truth? Had this girl really come to live there? Samantha ducked through the tunnel and came closer.

"Are you Nellie?" she asked brightly.

The girl looked surprised and very timid. "Yes, miss," she answered without stopping her work. Eddie had said Nellie was nine, but this girl seemed smaller than Samantha.

"Are you visiting the Rylands?" asked Samantha.

This time Nellie looked amused. "Oh, no, miss. I'm working here," she said.

Samantha was surprised. Eddie hadn't said a girl was coming to *work.* But it didn't matter. Samantha thought it would be wonderful to have a friend right next door. She remembered the cookie in her hand. "Would you like some gingerbread?" she asked. "It's just baked."

Nellie looked at the Rylands' house. "Oh, no, miss. I can't."

"Won't they let you?" asked Samantha.

"No, I don't think so, miss. I've got my job to do," Nellie answered.

"My name's Samantha. You don't have to call me 'miss.'" Samantha put her cookie and napkin down on a stone and reached for a piece of wet laundry. "I'll help you, Nellie. Then we can play."

"Oh, no, you shouldn't," Nellie said. She was

embarrassed, but there was nothing she could do to stop her new friend. So instead, she hurried to finish the job before anyone could see Samantha working.

When the last of the laundry was hung, Samantha grabbed Nellie's hand and pulled her toward the tunnel. "We can eat in here. Nobody will see us," Samantha said. The girls just fit into the hole in the hedge, and Nellie couldn't say no to the spicy smell of gingerbread.

"Why are you working here?" Samantha asked between bites.

Nellie didn't look at Samantha when she answered. "My father works in a factory in the city, and my mother does washing. But there's three of us children, you see, and it's not enough." She added quietly, "There wasn't enough food. And there wasn't enough coal."

Samantha's eyes were wide with disbelief. She was good at imagining castles and jungles and sailing ships, but she had never imagined hunger and cold. "You mean your parents sent you away? But that's awful!"

"Oh, no. It's better here. It really is," said Nellie. "The Rylands pay my family a dollar a week for the work I do. That's not as much as I earned in the factory, but in the factory I had to work every day but Sunday, until dark. And the air was so hot and dusty, I started coughing a lot. That's why my parents let me come here. The air is good, and I don't have to work so long, and I get good food." With one finger, she collected the last of the cookie crumbs. "Only I don't get to see my family much."

Samantha was shocked into silence, but only for a moment. "When do you go to school?" she asked.

"I've never been to school," Nellie said quietly.

Was it possible? This girl had never gone to school? Samantha's mind raced. "Nellie, I have an idea," she said. "We can meet here every day, and I'll teach you. The Rylands won't miss you for just a little while, and I'll teach you *everything.*"

Nellie's eyes glittered with excitement as the girls made plans. Then Samantha began talking about everyone she lived with and all the neighbors. By the time she'd told Nellie about Uncle Gard's automobile, they were both giggling.

The girls were interrupted by a familiar voice. "I see you, Samantha! I see you, Nellie! And you're really ugly. You're both so ugly, you'd scare a moose. You're so ugly—"

"Eddie, get out of here," Samantha snapped.

"I'm telling!"

Eddie started toward the house. Nellie looked frightened, but Samantha yelled "Eddie!" in a voice that made him think he'd better wait to hear what she had to say. "Eddie, if you tell anybody anything about us, I will take your new pocketknife and I will stuff it full of taffy."

Eddie stopped. He stared at Samantha. Then he put his hand over his back pocket to protect his knife. He began to back away from the girls. Finally, he ran away.

When he'd gone, Nellie jumped up. "I'd better get back to work," she said.

Samantha followed her out of the tunnel. "All right. But tomorrow we'll make a telephone. Mrs. Hawkins will give us two tin cans, and I can get a string. We'll string it through the hedge, where Eddie won't see it. Then we can talk whenever we want to. Oh, Nellie, we'll have the most wonderful time!"

Gone!

CHAPTER 4

By next Tuesday afternoon, Samantha's sampler read "ACTIONS SPEAK LOUDER THA." The sewing hour was almost over when there was a gentle knock on the parlor door.

"Come in," said Grandmary, and Jessie came in dressed to leave for home. She curtsied quickly and waited for Grandmary to speak.

Samantha thought Jessie always looked elegant. She was so tall and held her head so high. Jessie looked especially grand today. She was wearing a light brown summer coat that matched the color of her skin. But Samantha wondered why she was leaving so early.

"Yes, Jessie?" questioned Grandmary.

"Ma'am, I've just come to say I won't be coming back after today," Jessie said.

Samantha almost jumped out of her chair. "Jessie! Why?" she asked.

Grandmary silenced her with a look that said children should be seen and not heard. She spoke to Jessie. "Very well, Jessie. I'd like to thank you for your service. You have been a great help and a pleasure to us. We shall miss you very much."

Samantha was horrified. What was Grandmary saying? How could she just let Jessie go away like that?

"You can see Hawkins for your pay," continued Grandmary. "There will be a bonus for you."

Jessie curtsied again. "Thank you, ma'am." Before she left she stopped to smile at Samantha. "Be very good, Miss Samantha. You know I'll miss you."

Samantha was too stunned to answer. She watched Jessie go. Then her words rushed out. "Grandmary, why is Jessie leaving? And why did you let her?"

Grandmary's eyes never moved from the lacework in her hands. "Please sit down, Samantha," she said. "A young lady must not ask questions of her elders. This is Jessie's business."

Samantha sat down, but she could only fidget with her sewing. It seemed as if every stitch she put in her sampler had to be pulled out again. She didn't understand. Why would Jessie leave without explaining?

At last the sewing hour was over. Samantha curtsied quickly when Grandmary excused her. Then she rushed out of the parlor to find Mrs. Hawkins, the cook.

There was never any problem finding Mrs. Hawkins. She was always in the kitchen. And the kitchen was always filled with the wonderful smells of Mrs. Hawkins's cooking. Today she stood by the big wooden table in the center of the room, rolling pastry for meat pie. She wasn't surprised to see Samantha. The kitchen was one of Samantha's favorite places. She came there often to talk and to eat the treats Mrs. Hawkins saved for her.

"Hello, love," Mrs. Hawkins said. "Why are you rushing so? Sit down now and tell me what's the matter. You look like thunder."

Samantha flopped herself down on a chair. "Jessie's gone away," she said.

"Yes, dear, I know."

Mrs. Hawkins knew? Everybody knew but Samantha! She brushed away a fly that buzzed in from the open windows. "But why?" she asked. "Grandmary didn't even try to stop her!"

"Now, now, love. You must not fret about it," Mrs. Hawkins said. She took an onion from a bunch hanging by the door and began to peel it. "There are some things you just don't understand. Don't you think your Grandmary knows best?"

How could Samantha possibly know if Grandmary knew best? How could she know if anybody knew best? She didn't know what anybody knew!

She pushed back her chair and hurried from the kitchen to the butler's pantry. She hoped Hawkins would be there, and he was. Hawkins was whistling softly and polishing silver. He pulled out a chair for Samantha. He was used to her popping up in strange places. They had their best talks when Samantha followed him around on his jobs, waxing furniture, beating the carpets, or washing the windows in Grandmary's big house. Now Hawkins handed Samantha a polishing cloth. He knew how much easier it is to talk when your hands are busy.

Samantha rubbed at a sugar bowl. "Jessie's gone," she said.

"I know," said Hawkins. Samantha wasn't surprised.

"Nobody will tell me why," Samantha went on.

Hawkins smiled, and his eyes were understanding. But when he spoke, it didn't help much. "Believe me, Miss Samantha, Jessie's fine," he said. "I know it isn't easy, but sometimes, when you're young, you just have to trust."

Samantha didn't feel much like talking anymore. She pushed back the sugar bowl and cloth, straightened her chair, and slowly left the pantry. As she shuffled past the parlor, Grandmary called, "Samantha."

"Yes, ma'am?"

"I have been very pleased with your efforts these past weeks," Grandmary said. "If you go upstairs, you will find something on your bed."

For a minute Samantha forgot about Jessie's leaving. She even forgot to say thank you as she ran up the stairs two at a time. Inside her room, Samantha stopped short. There in the middle of her bed was a doll dressed in shining blue silk. "Oh, Lydia," Samantha whispered. She picked the doll up gently. Then she hugged her very close.

Night Visit

CHAPTER 5

The next morning, Samantha brought Lydia to meet Nellie in the tunnel. But when she saw how Nellie's eyes glowed and how gently she touched Lydia's dress, Samantha wondered if she had been wrong to bring the doll. Nellie had never owned a doll, not even a simple doll, and certainly not a doll as beautiful as Lydia.

"It's all right if you play with her," Samantha said. "Look. Her hat can come off and her dress even has little buttons."

While Nellie cradled Lydia, Samantha told her what had happened.

"Jessie left, and nobody will tell me why," Samantha said.

Nellie didn't answer. She was buttoning the tiny buttons.

"I think I know, though," Samantha continued. "I think she's going to be an actress."

Nellie carefully removed Lydia's hat and turned it over in her hand.

"She'll be famous," Samantha went on. "And one day she'll come back here, and we'll go to see her. And she'll take you and me to meet all the actors and actresses. Only you and me, out of the whole town. Because we were her friends."

Nellie still had nothing to say. Now she was looking at the doll's tiny leather shoes.

In the days that followed, Samantha came up with several reasons for Jessie's leaving. Maybe Jessie had gone to New Orleans with Lincoln, to be a singer there. Jessie had a beautiful voice. Or the President might have asked her to be a spy in Europe. She'd sew elegant clothes for kings and queens and learn their secrets. Or maybe her brother had been kidnapped and taken to South America, and Jessie was going to rescue him.

Then one day Nellie had a suggestion. "Maybe she's got a baby," Nellie said.

Samantha was startled. "Why would she do that?"

"Lots of people do," Nellie said. "They like babies."

Samantha had to agree. "Jessie loves babies."

"Well then?"

Samantha was annoyed. Nellie's idea wasn't half as exciting as any of hers. But it was too sensible to be ignored. "Why wouldn't Grandmary tell me if it was a baby?" asked Samantha.

Nellie shrugged. "Grown-ups don't like to talk about babies coming."

Samantha had to agree. "I asked Grandmary about babies once, and she said it wasn't a proper subject for young girls."

Nellie nodded in understanding.

"I asked Mrs. Hawkins, and she said the stork brings babies. But she wouldn't talk about it anymore," Samantha continued.

"I don't think it's true anyway," said Nellie. "When my baby sister came, the midwife was at our building. My other sister and I had to go out with my uncle. When we got back, my baby sister was there and the midwife was fixing tea for my mother. But there wasn't any stork anywhere."

Samantha was puzzled. "What's a midwife?" she asked.

"She's a lady who visits whenever a new baby comes," Nellie answered. "My uncle said she brings the baby in her little black bag. But I looked in, and the bag was full of things like doctors have. There wouldn't be any room for a baby in there."

"Nellie, we've just *got* to find out what happened to Jessie," said Samantha. "If we just knew where she lived, we could ask Lincoln. He must know where she is."

"I know where she lives," said Nellie.

Samantha's eyes were wide with surprise. "You do?"

Nellie nodded. "A woman across the street from Jessie makes an herb tea that cures headaches. One day Mrs. Ryland wanted some, so she sent me home with Jessie to get it. I can show you."

Samantha hugged her. "Oh, Nellie, that's perfect! Only we can't go in the daytime. They'd stop us for sure. We'll go tonight. When everyone's in bed, I'll sneak down the back stairs and meet you right here in the tunnel. Look out your window and watch my house. Grandmary always turns out the gas lamps just before she goes to bed. That's how you'll know it's all right for me to come down and meet you."

Nellie agreed. She knew that no one at the Ryland house would even notice if she went out after she had finished her evening chores.

Samantha had always thought the nighttime was very quiet, but that night, noises seemed to come from everywhere. The crickets were making a terrible racket. The bushes and trees rustled as though they were hiding wild animals, and dogs barked all around. Samantha closed the back door carefully and hurried to the tunnel to find Nellie.

The two girls held hands and started out of the yard and up the street. As long as they were on familiar streets, where gas lamps glowed with a friendly light, they thought their adventure was grand and very exciting. But after they crossed the railroad tracks, the streets got dark and narrow. The houses were dark, too, and very small. Somewhere there was loud music and noisy laughter, and once in a while there was shouting. Nellie squeezed Samantha's hand so tightly that Samantha couldn't have let go if she'd wanted to. But she certainly didn't want to. She was just as frightened as her friend was. *Maybe we shouldn't have come at all,* she thought. But she didn't say that to Nellie. She wanted to be brave.

"Are you sure you know the way?" Samantha whispered.

"I—I think so." Nellie's voice was shaky. "It's not much farther now."

Samantha looked at the drab houses they were passing. Even in the dark she could tell there wasn't much grass in front, and there was very little room for flowers. "Why does Jessie live here?" she asked.

"This is the colored part of town," Nellie answered.

"You mean Jessie *has* to live here?" Samantha asked.

Nellie looked at her. Samantha was smart about so many things that Nellie was always surprised at what her friend didn't know. "Yes, of course," Nellie said.

"Why?" asked Samantha.

"I don't know," Nellie said. "It's just the way grown-ups do things." Her face lit up with relief. "There it is," she said. The soft glow of a kerosene lamp shone from a window, and the girls rushed to the wall beneath it. They huddled there for a minute, panting.

"Aren't you going to knock on the door?" Nellie whispered.

Samantha suddenly lost her nerve. "What if it's not the right house after all?" she said. "Or what if Jessie went away with Lincoln, and somebody else lives there now?"

"Well, we can look in the window," said Nellie. "I'll get down and you can get on my back. Then you can see in."

"No, I'm stronger," answered Samantha. "You get on my back."

Samantha got on her hands and knees. Nellie stepped carefully onto her back. She held tight to the windowsill and looked over. "Oh, Samantha," she whispered. "Jessie's there . . . and Lincoln, too, and . . . and . . ."

"What?"

"There's a cradle."

At just that moment Jessie looked up. She shrieked at the face she saw peering in at her. Nellie tried to duck, but she lost her balance and fell over, kicking Samantha in the ribs as she went. So it was a tangle of arms and legs and frightened faces that Lincoln found when he came outside the house. He laughed out loud.

Inside, Jessie brushed the girls' dresses. "I declare, Miss Samantha, I think I'll spend the rest of my life straightening you up after mischief," she chuckled. "What on earth are you doing here at such a time of night? Where's Hawkins?"

The girls looked at one another shyly. Then Samantha spoke. "We came by ourselves, Jessie. We didn't know what had happened to you, and no one would tell us."

Jessie's smile melted and she put her arms around Samantha. "My poor child," she said. "I'm sorry. I never dreamed you'd worry. But you see, I'm fine." She stood back and smiled proudly. "And now, come see my treasure." She went to the cradle and lifted out a tiny blanketed bundle. She brought it over to the girls and announced, "This is Nathaniel."

Wrapped in the blanket was the tiniest person Samantha had ever seen. His skin was the same fine brown as his mother's, and his head was covered with soft black curls. His cheeks were so round and soft that Samantha couldn't resist reaching out to touch them. When his tiny pink mouth opened and closed, she was sure he smiled at her. "Oh, Jessie," she breathed. "He's beautiful."

Jessie beamed and tucked the baby back in his cradle with a kiss. "But you see why I couldn't stay at your grandmother's," she said, turning back to the girls. "Lincoln's gone most of the time, working. I've got to be here to take care of Nathaniel. But don't worry, Miss Samantha. I'll come to see you often. And I'll bring Nathaniel, too." She hugged Samantha quickly. Then she hustled the girls to the door. "Now Lincoln is going to take you home. If your grandmother finds out you're gone, she'll have your hide and mine, too."

The way home seemed much shorter with Lincoln's strong hands to guide them. Nellie and Samantha crept into their houses without making a sound. Samantha tiptoed quickly up the stairs and back into her room. She hurried to unbutton her shoes and take off her stockings. She hung her dress in the tall wooden wardrobe, unbuttoned her underwaist, and slipped her long nightgown over her head. Her nightgown had never felt so soft and comforting. Her bed had never smelled so sweet or been so welcome. She held Lydia very close and fell asleep.

A Sense of Value

CHAPTER 6

Two days later, Samantha tugged on the string of her tin-can telephone. She and Nellie had tied bells to both ends of the telephone, so that they could signal one another when they wanted to talk. But today Nellie didn't answer.

Samantha tugged again, but still there was no answer. She crawled through the tunnel. There was no sign of Nellie. Instead, Eddie Ryland stood there pulling gum out of his mouth in long strings and then stuffing it back in again.

"I know something you don't know," Eddie said. He looked pleased with himself, and that worried Samantha. She waited.

"Nellie is going away," Eddie said.

Samantha felt as though she'd been hit. "What are you talking about, Eddie?"

"Our driver's taking her back to the city. She's sick, and my mother says she's not strong enough to work. She's waiting in the kitchen. Mother says next time we'll get an immigrant woman who can last longer."

Samantha wanted more than anything to punch Eddie in the nose. But she knew she couldn't. She knew that even if she were a boy, she couldn't punch Eddie in the nose. Certainly a grown-up person would not punch Eddie in the nose. A grown-up person probably would not have reached out and shoved Eddie's chewing gum into his hair either. But Samantha did. After all, she was only nine, and that is only half grown-up. Then she rushed to her friend, leaving Eddie howling and trying to pull the sticky mess out of his curls.

In the Rylands' kitchen, Nellie sat on a wooden chair, swinging her legs and staring at her belongings. They were tied in a shawl at her feet.

"Nellie, are you sick?" Samantha asked.

Nellie looked up. "No, I'm not sick," she said. "But I still cough sometimes. Mrs. Ryland is afraid I'll get sick and be a bother, so she's sending me back."

"But Nellie, will you have to go to work in the

factory again? You'll get sick if you go back. And what will I do without you?"

Nellie had started to cry. "It'll be all right, Samantha. Really it will. Only I'll miss you so much."

Samantha couldn't stand to see Nellie crying. "Wait a minute, I'll be right back," she said. She dashed across the yard and into her own kitchen.

"Mrs. Hawkins!" Samantha cried breathlessly. "Mrs. Hawkins, they're sending Nellie away, and her family doesn't have enough food. We have to give them something."

Mrs. Hawkins would have been quick to help even without Samantha's begging. In a few minutes she had packed a basket with a pie and fruit, some food in tin cans, and a ham. Samantha ran back to the Rylands' kitchen carrying the basket—and something else. She put the basket at Nellie's feet. Then she placed Lydia in her arms.

"Here, Nellie. You take Lydia," Samantha said. "She'll be your friend." Samantha hugged Nellie and stayed with her until the Rylands' driver came.

Later that afternoon, Uncle Gard and Cornelia were having tea with Grandmary. Samantha was there, too, but she was not playing and laughing with Uncle Gard. She was sitting in her chair, working on her sampler, because even *that* was better than talking to grown-ups. Samantha was feeling very angry with grown-ups. Grown-ups took her friends away and never even told her why. So she sat and stabbed the needle at her sampler, and everyone wondered why Samantha was in such a bad mood.

Then suddenly, even before she knew she was going to, Samantha blurted out, "I know why Jessie left."

Grandmary looked surprised. "You do?"

"Yes. She has a baby," Samantha said.

Now Grandmary was really surprised. "How do you know that?" she asked.

"Nellie and I went to her house at night, and we saw." Samantha was sure Grandmary would punish her now.

But Grandmary looked more troubled than angry. "You were very wrong to do that, Samantha," she said.

"Well, you were very wrong not to tell me," said Samantha. She was not feeling very respectful.

Grandmary took in her breath sharply. She

looked at Uncle Gard and Cornelia for help. But they said nothing.

Grandmary put her teacup down and nodded slowly. "Yes, Samantha, I think you are right. I should have told you," she said.

The room was very quiet. Samantha felt pleased and relieved. "Well, can Jessie come back?" she asked.

"Now, Samantha, you know she has to take care of the baby."

"But she could bring him with her," said Samantha. "He wouldn't bother anybody."

Grandmary looked thoughtful. "Well, I hadn't thought about that. But I suppose if Jessie wants to, and Mrs. Hawkins doesn't object . . ." As if anyone could possibly imagine Mrs. Hawkins objecting to Nathaniel!

"Oh, thank you, Grandmary!" Samantha almost shouted. But Grandmary wasn't used to making mistakes, and she was feeling embarrassed. She changed the subject. "You don't have your doll today, Samantha. Are you tired of her already?"

Samantha felt her face turn hot. "No. I lost her."

"You *lost* her?" Grandmary was upset. "My dear

Samantha, how are you ever going to grow into a proper young lady? I try and I try to give you a sense of value and you—"

"I think Sam's sense of value is just fine, Mother," Uncle Gard interrupted quietly. "She gave the doll to Nellie. Mrs. Hawkins told me."

Grandmary stopped short. She looked at Uncle Gard, and then she looked at Samantha. Then she nodded slowly. "Yes," she said. "Yes, I think Samantha's sense of value is just fine indeed."

Samantha ran to her grandmother.

"Grandmary, we've got to help Nellie's family. They don't have enough food and they don't have enough coal. Can we help them? Please?"

Grandmary's eyebrows went up, and then she threw back her head and laughed. "Yes, Samantha. If you care enough to give up your finest treasure, then we can find a way to help Nellie's family." She gave Samantha a proud smile. "You really are quite a fine young lady, Samantha Parkington," she said as she opened her arms to fold Samantha in a hug as warm as summer sunshine.

Notes and Knee Bends

CHAPTER 7

For the rest of the summer, Samantha avoided going to the lilac tunnel in her backyard. Playing there alone made her miss Nellie. When school started in the fall, Samantha was especially happy to see her friends every day.

Something poked Samantha in the back one bright September morning as she sat in class. She jumped slightly, but she didn't look up. Samantha knew the signal. It was from Helen.

Helen Whitney had the desk behind Samantha's. Both desks were like all the other desks in the classroom at Miss Crampton's Academy for Girls. Their iron sides were molded in lacy swirls and curls. And one particular curl was just the right size for holding notes.

Talking in class was not allowed at Miss Crampton's, so when Helen had something to tell

Samantha, she would write it on a small piece of paper. Then she would roll the paper up, stick it in the proper iron curl, and poke Samantha in the back with her pencil. Samantha would wait until Miss Stevens wasn't looking, and then drop her hand back and pull out the note. Once she caught her finger in the iron swirls and barely got it loose before Miss Stevens turned around. But usually the system worked wonderfully.

Now Samantha waited until the teacher's back was turned. She reached for the note. It said:

What the dickens does "la gorge" mean?

Samantha looked up quickly, squashed the note small, and shoved it into her pocket. It would be bad enough to be caught passing notes in school. She couldn't imagine what would happen if she were caught with a note that said *the dickens.* Didn't Helen have enough sense not to write almost-swear-words?

There wasn't enough time for Samantha to answer Helen's note. Miss Stevens had already finished writing a long list of French words on the blackboard. Now she turned around and faced the class. And she looked straight at Helen.

"Helen, will you please tell us what *la gorge* means?" Miss Stevens asked.

Samantha tried to give Helen a clue. "A-a-ahemm," she cleared her throat rather loudly. Miss Stevens stared at her, then looked back at Helen.

Helen didn't answer, so Samantha tried again. She rubbed the back of her neck.

"Samantha, are you well?" asked Miss Stevens. She was looking at Samantha through gold-rimmed spectacles that seemed to see everything. She looked as if she had a pretty good idea of what was going on.

"Yes, ma'am," said Samantha softly. She folded her hands on her desk. Helen would have to answer on her own.

"Is it the neck?" squeaked Helen uncertainly.

"No, Helen, it is not," said Miss Stevens. She looked around the room. Edith Eddleton stretched her hand high in the air, and Miss Stevens called on her.

"La gorge," said Edith smugly, "means the throat."

"That is correct," said Miss Stevens, and Edith gloated. Samantha could just imagine Edith keeping score in her head: "me—107; everyone else—0." Edith was smart, but not as smart as she thought she was. Probably no one on earth was as smart as Edith Eddleton thought she was.

The class was just finishing the list of words on the blackboard when the lunch bell rang. The girls stood beside their desks. They waited until Miss Stevens nodded for them to go and get their lunch boxes from the cloakroom. Then they filed quietly out the door.

The day was warm, so the girls could eat outside on the benches in the yard. Helen, Ida Dean, and Ruth Adams waited for Samantha at their usual spot. Samantha squirmed as she sat down next to them. Her legs itched from the long flannel underwear that was tucked under her stockings. But she had to wear it, whether the days were warm or cold. Grandmary said flannel underwear kept children from getting consumption, and she insisted that Samantha put it on at the beginning of September.

"Do you think Miss Crampton will make us do arm stretches today?" Ida asked between bites of her chopped olive sandwich. Miss Crampton was Head of the Academy, and she was very serious about exercise. At one o'clock every day she came to the classroom to lead the girls in exercises. "If she makes us do fifty arm stretches, I'm going to faint," Ida added with a sigh.

"At least arm stretches are better than knee bends," answered Helen. "I hate knee bends. I think Miss Crampton is trying for the world record in knee bends."

"It could be worse," said Ruth. "At my cousin's school they have to practice swimming. But they don't have any water. They have to hang with big ropes around their waists. Then they have to kick and paddle. Just hanging in the air like that."

Ida looked at her in disbelief. "Oh, they never!" she gasped.

Ruth nodded importantly. "I swear it. They do." And she licked jelly neatly off her fingers.

The girls were quiet for a moment, all giving silent thanks for the swimming hole in Mount Bedford. At least they could learn to swim in *real* water. "Maybe knee bends aren't so bad after all," Ida finally said.

Samantha took a gingerbread cookie out of her lunchbox and grew quiet while the other girls talked on. Every time she had gingerbread, Samantha thought about Nellie. Samantha had given Nellie her first taste of gingerbread. Now Samantha wondered about her friend, who had been back in New York for two months. Samantha remembered all the things Nellie had told her about her life in the city, and she worried.

Nellie had said her whole family—all five of them—lived in one room in a crowded building. There was only one window in the room, and the air always smelled bad. In the summer the room was very hot, and in the winter it was terribly cold. There was a little stove for cooking, but there was never enough coal to make the room warm. And Nellie had said they were nearly always hungry, because there wasn't enough money.

Samantha remembered all the things Nellie had told her, and the gingerbread tasted dry in her mouth.

As she swallowed the last of her milk, Samantha's thoughts were jerked back to the schoolyard by the ringing of Miss Crampton's bell. She hurried to get in line with the other girls. They all marched back inside to face another afternoon beginning with Miss Crampton's knee bends.

Nellie

CHAPTER 8

On Saturday morning Samantha was getting dressed when there was a sharp knock at her door. Elsa leaned her head in. "You have company, miss," she said. Elsa looked annoyed at having to bother with Samantha's company. "Your grandmother said to tell you it's a friend. She's in the parlor." Samantha was surprised. She had lots of friends who came to play, but Grandmary would never tell any of them to wait in the parlor. The parlor was only for grown-up visitors. Samantha hurried downstairs. She stopped in the hall to straighten her dress, then slowly opened the parlor door and looked around. At first she thought the room was empty. Then she saw a wide blue bow just peeking over the back of the green velvet chair. That was enough.

"Nellie!" Samantha yelled. She ran around the chair

and hugged the girl who jumped up to meet her. Nellie was laughing.

"Oh, Nellie, it's really you! You're all right!" Samantha stood back and looked at her friend. "Are you back at the Rylands'?" she asked.

"Oh, no, it's much better," Nellie said. Her eyes were sparkling. "It was your grandmother, Samantha. She talked to Mrs. Van Sicklen, and Mrs. Van Sicklen hired my mother and father. Dad will be her driver. He'll take care of the horses and the garden. Mam will cook and clean and do laundry. And Bridget and Jenny and I will help." Nellie bounced with excitement. She looked as if she had a grand surprise. "And guess what, Samantha? We get to *live* there! All of us! We really do! In the rooms over the carriage house. Isn't that wonderful?"

Samantha grabbed Nellie's hands and danced with her around the parlor. "Oh, Nellie! You'll live only two houses away. We can play every single day when I get home from school."

Nellie stopped. Only her eyes danced now. She leaned over as if to tell a secret. "Samantha," she said in an excited half-whisper, "I'm going to go to school, too.

Mrs. Van Sicklen told your grandmother I could."
Nellie jumped a little jump and clapped her hands. "What do you think of that?"

Samantha hugged her. "Oh, Nellie, that *is* wonderful. It's just wonderful! I'm so glad you're back!" Samantha swung Nellie around in a circle and then started toward the door. "Come on," she called, "maybe Mrs. Hawkins will give us some gingerbread!"

Monday morning Samantha led a strange parade down the hill, across Main Street, and into the Mount Bedford Public School. She walked tall and proud, dressed in her best gray dress. Nellie walked next to her, skipping little excited skips now and then. Jenny and Bridget, Nellie's little sisters, followed behind. They squeezed each other's hands and walked very quietly.

Bridget was seven and Jenny was six. They would both start in the first grade. They looked shy and scared as they tiptoed into their classroom.

Then Samantha led Nellie to the second grade classroom. Nellie would start there because she knew her letters and she could read a little, even though she had never been to school before. In the dim hallway, facing the tall oak door, Nellie looked frightened. She twisted her hand in her dress and looked at Samantha for help. "Everything will be fine, you'll see," Samantha said. "Remember, I'll meet you on the front steps when school's over."

Nellie took a deep breath and stepped into her classroom. Samantha hurried out of the building and ran the two blocks to Miss Crampton's.

All day long Samantha worried about Nellie. During morning exercises she wished she had taught Nellie the Oath of Allegiance. She knew they would be saying it in the public school. Did Nellie know it? Did she know the hymns they would sing?

At lunchtime, as Samantha ate her watercress sandwich, she remembered the lard pails Nellie and her sisters had carried as lunchboxes. She wished she had looked inside. She wasn't sure they had enough to eat. At least she could have given them her cookies.

During penmanship class, Samantha practiced S's and Q's and thought that she should have stayed longer with Nellie. Would someone help her find the pencil sharpener? Would there be someone to show her where the bathroom was?

By three o'clock Samantha was almost bursting to know how Nellie had gotten along. She ran the two blocks to the public school and climbed the front steps two at a time. Jenny and Bridget began jumping up and down the minute they saw her. Both of them talked at once.

"There are thirty desks in our room, Samantha. I can count to thirty," Bridget said.

"I have my own desk," Jenny added.

"We put our lunches in the clock room," Bridget continued.

"No, Bridget, it's not a clock room, it's a *cloak* room," said Samantha.

"We have books, see?" Jenny held up three books strapped together with a leather belt.

"That's nice, Jenny," said Samantha. "But where's Nellie? Why isn't she here?"

The little girls looked at each other and shrugged. "We don't know. We haven't seen her."

Samantha looked around. All the other boys and girls were on their way home. Samantha saw Eddie

Ryland pulling Carrie Wilson's hair ribbon off and running down the street with it. But there was no sign of Nellie. Where could she be?

Then Samantha saw her. Nellie was huddled by the bushes near the foot of the steps. She was sitting on her heels with her head in her hands. And she was crying.

The three girls ran down the steps and crouched next to Nellie. Jenny and Bridget began patting their sister's back and stroking her hair. Samantha put her arm around Nellie. "What is it? What's the matter?" she asked.

"I can't do it, Samantha," Nellie sobbed. "I'm too old to start school. I can't do it."

"But Nellie, what happened?"

"The children all laughed at me because I'm big and I'm just in second grade," said Nellie as she lifted her tear-stained face. "The teacher made me sit at the back of the room. And she got mad at me when I couldn't get the right answer. She asked me where the Atlantic Ocean was, and I was just so scared that I forgot. Then the children laughed even more." Nellie shuddered with a little sob. "They called me 'ragbag.' And one time when a boy passed my desk, he leaned over and whispered 'dummy.'" Nellie hid her face in her lap again. "Oh, Samantha, I can't go back tomorrow," she sobbed.

"Yes, you can, Nellie," Samantha said firmly. She was very angry. And when Samantha was angry, she was not likely to sit still.

"Nellie, do you know the way home by yourself?" Samantha asked. Nellie nodded. "Well then, you take Jenny and Bridget home. I have to do something. Dry your eyes. It's going to be all right. I promise you it's going to be all right."

Nellie rubbed her hand over her eyes and sniffed loudly. But she got up, took her sisters' hands, and started home. Samantha marched back to Miss Crampton's Academy.

Mount Better School

CHAPTER 9

iss Stevens was at her desk. She was busy writing something, but she stopped when she saw Samantha. "Can I help you, Samantha?" she asked.

"Yes, Miss Stevens," answered Samantha. She did not know quite how to begin. At last she said, "I have a friend, and she's just started school. She's nine, but she never went to school because she had to work in a factory. She's in the second grade." Samantha stopped and watched Miss Stevens closely to see if she would think this was funny. But Miss Stevens didn't look as if she thought there was anything funny at all.

Samantha went on. "The children tease her and the teacher is mean. She thinks my friend isn't very smart. But she *is* smart, Miss Stevens. She just needs help."

Miss Stevens nodded, so Samantha kept talking.

"I could teach her, but I don't know what she needs to learn." She looked at Miss Stevens hopefully. "Can you help us?"

Miss Stevens looked thoughtful. "You are a very good friend, Samantha. I think you will be a good teacher, too. Come sit down."

Samantha sat on the chair next to her teacher's desk, and Miss Stevens went to a bookshelf at the side of the room. She came back with four books. "These are the second grade books," she said. "There's a speller, a reader, an arithmetic book, and a geography book." Miss Stevens began writing in the books with a pencil. "I'm marking parts in each of them. Do you think you can help your friend learn them?"

"Yes, Miss Stevens," Samantha said.

"Good," Miss Stevens replied. "Now, stop and see me after school on Friday. Tell me how much your friend has done, and I will help you plan for the following week. It's going to mean quite a bit of work, Samantha. Do you think you can do it?"

"Oh, yes. We can do it!" Samantha stood up, reached for the books, and dashed out of the classroom. She ran most of the way home. Samantha was so eager to get started that she almost forgot to curtsy when she burst into Grandmary's sitting room. She remembered and bobbed quickly, just in time to avoid her grandmother's frown.

"Grandmary, may I start a school?" Samantha asked in a rush.

Even though Grandmary was used to the unexpected from Samantha, she could still be surprised. She raised an eyebrow and looked at her granddaughter. "Why, Samantha, are you quite sure you've learned all that Miss Stevens has to teach you?"

Samantha tried to explain. "Grandmary, I want to start a school for Nellie. She's having a terrible time at the public school. The teacher is mean to her, and the children tease her because she's just in second grade. But if I helped her, she could move up to the third grade really fast. I just know she could."

Grandmary thought for a minute before she answered. "I'm glad that you are willing to help Nellie," Grandmary said. "But you must not take up too much of her time, Samantha. Nellie has duties at the Van Sicklens' house, and I know you would not want her to neglect any of them."

"I won't take too much time, I promise," said Samantha. "And we'll be so quiet, you won't even know we're here." A little smile crept around Grandmary's mouth, and Samantha knew she had won.

"Very well," said Grandmary. "I guess it won't do any harm."

"Thank you, Grandmary," said Samantha as she hugged her grandmother quickly. Then she hurried out of the room to get her school ready.

It was past four o'clock when Samantha went into the Van Sicklens' backyard looking for Nellie. Samantha couldn't see anyone around, but she could hear someone in the laundry room. She peeked inside and saw Nellie ironing clothes. Nellie worked at a table in the middle of the room. Next to her, three irons sat on a small coal stove. Nellie was sweating with the heat. She put the iron she was using back on the stove and picked up a hot one before she noticed Samantha. Her face brightened when she saw her friend.

"Can you come over to my house?" asked Samantha.

"Oh, not now," Nellie said as she wiped her face

with the corner of her apron. "I have to finish the ironing first. But I'm pretty near done." She looked down at her basket. "I can come in about a half-hour."

"All right," Samantha said. "I'll wait for you on my back steps." She walked back to her house and sat with a book until she saw Nellie coming through the hedge.

Nellie was carrying Lydia. The beautiful doll was no longer quite so fine. Her dress was wrinkled and worn because she had been held so often. Her hair was mussed because Nellie hugged her so tightly at night. Her china hands and face were dirty because Nellie took her with her wherever she could. Samantha looked at Lydia and knew she had been loved.

"Come on, Nellie. I have something to show you," she said.

Together, the two girls went inside. In the hallway next to the kitchen, Samantha opened a door that led to a curving stairway. She started up, and Nellie followed. The stairs ended on the second floor, at the back of Grandmary's house. Samantha opened another door. The steps were narrower now. They ended in the attic. Samantha led the way down a narrow hall, past Elsa's room and Jessie's sewing room, to a third stairway. These steps were very steep, and sunlight poured down from above them.

As the girls climbed, Nellie's heart beat faster. She knew where they were now. Samantha was taking her to the small tower that rose above her house and made it look like a palace. Nellie held her breath as she followed Samantha up.

And suddenly they were there—in a tiny room above the world. There was a window in each of the four walls, and Nellie hurried to peer out of each one in turn. She could see all the way down the hill to School Street. She could see the Rylands' house and the Van Sicklens'. And she could see over the trees on the hill. Nellie had never been up so high before. She thought it felt like flying.

When she turned around, Nellie saw that the room was special inside, too. Samantha's small blackboard was there, standing on wooden legs like an easel. There were cushions to sit on and books stacked neatly against one wall. And there was a small jar of dried white beans.

Nellie was amazed. "Samantha, what . . . ?"

"Here, sit down. We're going to get you out of the

second grade, Nellie. Put Lydia on the window seat and let's get started." Samantha opened a book to the place Miss Stevens had marked. "Why don't you start reading there, and when you come to a word you don't know, I'll write it on the blackboard so you can practice it."

Nellie read two pages and Samantha wrote eleven words on the blackboard. Nellie copied them in her copybook to take home and study.

Next they worked on penmanship. Samantha thought this might be difficult for Nellie. She remembered how hard it had been to make her own letters small enough, and how she had worked to get all the curls in the right places. But Nellie was fascinated by the letters. She loved the fancy look of them. Even though her first letters were crooked, she kept trying and trying to make them beautiful. Finally it was Samantha who said it was time to stop. They would have to go on to arithmetic.

Samantha spilled some beans out of the jar and onto the floor. She began arranging them in rows. "All right, Nellie, here are seven beans and here are five," she said. "Now, if you add them together—"

"Twelve," Nellie interrupted.

Samantha looked up, startled. She moved more beans into place. "Fourteen and nine," she said.

"Twenty-three," said Nellie, without bothering to count the beans.

Samantha scooped the beans back into the jar and said, "Seventeen and fifteen."

"Thirty-two," Nellie answered promptly.

Samantha sat back on her heels and stared at Nellie. "How did you know that?"

Nellie shrugged. "Lots of times in the city I did the shopping for Mam. I usually had just about a dollar, and I had to get food for all of us. I had to know how many pennies things cost. I had to know how many pennies I had left. And I had to know fast."

Samantha nodded slowly. She didn't want to think about Nellie counting pennies for food. She shoved the bean jar into a corner. "It's getting too late to look at the geography book now. We'll have to save that for another day," she said.

As the girls were stacking the books and getting ready to leave, Samantha had a thought.

"You know, Nellie," she said, "we should have a name for our school. I think we should call it the Mount Better School." Her smile had mischief in it as she looked at Nellie. "We've got better students than the Mount Bedford School."

A grin flashed across Nellie's face. "We've got better teachers, too," she said.

The Contest

CHAPTER 10

At school the next morning, Miss Crampton made an announcement.

"The Mount Bedford Ladies Club will be sponsoring the Young People's Speaking Contest again this year. The contest will be held on October fifth in the Mount Bedford Opera House. This year's subject is 'Progress in America.'

"Students from Lessing's Boys School and from the public elementary school will compete in the contest," Miss Crampton continued. "Our own Academy has been asked to send two girls to take part. In order to choose those two girls, we shall have a contest of our own three weeks from today. Each of you will prepare and present a speech. Miss Stevens and I shall choose the two best speeches.

"Think very carefully about progress in America,"

Miss Crampton went on. "Think of all the inventions that have changed our lives—the telephone, the steam engine, electric lights, and so many more. Talk to your parents and read books to get ideas. You have just three weeks to work on your speeches. You should begin today. And remember, I expect excellence."

By the time Miss Crampton finished, all the girls were thinking hard. And by lunchtime everyone was buzzing about the speaking contest.

"If you win," said Helen, "the mayor gives you the medal. Right up on the stage with everybody watching."

"It wouldn't matter if the *President* gave me a medal," said Ida glumly. "I get so nervous in front of people, I can hardly remember my name. I could never give a speech in public."

"You get your name in the paper if you win, too," Helen added.

"I would probably just faint and fall off the stage onto the mayor," said Ida. "And my parents would be so embarrassed, they'd have to leave town."

"I don't get nervous," said Ruth, "but I don't know enough big words to win. Judges always like big words."

"I'm going to keep smelling salts in my pocket,"

said Ida. "Remember them if I faint."

"Samantha's going to win," said one of the other girls. "Her essays are always the best, and she won't be scared on the stage."

Samantha shrugged modestly. "I wish I *could* win," she said. She knew she would certainly try. Wouldn't it be wonderful to be up on that stage and feel that medal in her hand?

"Edith Eddleton might win, though." It was Ruth speaking. Ruth was Samantha's friend, but she was an honest friend. "Edith knows more big words than the rest of us put together. And she's not scared of anything."

The other girls groaned. Helen made a face. "Ruth," she said, "just be quiet and eat your sandwich."

At three o'clock, Nellie and her sisters waited for Samantha on the front steps of Mount Bedford Public School. This afternoon there were no tears.

"How was it, Nellie?" called Samantha as the three bounded down the steps.

"It wasn't too bad," answered Nellie. Bridget took

Samantha's hand, and the girls started home.

"Did they tease you?" Samantha asked.

"They did some," said Nellie, trying to slow Jenny down. "But I didn't mind so much. The teacher mostly left me alone."

"Can you come to Mount Better School today?" asked Samantha.

Nellie looked uncertainly at Samantha. "I have to clean the parlor and sweep the mats," she said. "But if I get the table set right away, I can come for a little while before I have to serve dinner."

Just then Edith Eddleton came riding past on her bicycle. She looked at the girls and stopped. "Samantha Parkington, does your grandmother know you're walking home with *servant* girls?"

Samantha was shocked. "What are you talking about?"

Edith was only too glad to go on. "Those are Mrs. Van Sicklen's servants. I know *my* mother doesn't want *me* to spend time with them. But then, I guess some people just aren't very particular." And Edith climbed back on her bicycle and pedaled away.

Nellie's face got very red. For once Samantha was

speechless. She grabbed Bridget's hand tightly and marched up the sidewalk with long, angry steps. "You know, Nellie," Samantha finally said, "Edith Eddleton is even nastier than Eddie Ryland!"

That evening, Samantha had dinner with Grandmary. Samantha always loved the glitter of the silver and the crystal in the dining room. She loved the little silver bell Grandmary let her ring to tell Mrs. Hawkins to clear the table and bring dessert. She loved the special grown-up time she shared with Grandmary.

Of course, such a grown-up dinner wasn't easy. Samantha had to use her very best manners. She sat very straight and kept her napkin in her lap. She tilted her soup spoon away from her in her soup plate. She never spilled or dropped a crumb. She kept her elbows close to her sides, and she tried not to speak until she was spoken to.

Samantha waited until Grandmary asked her about school before she told about the speaking contest. "What do you think is the best sign of progress in America, Grandmary?" Samantha asked.

Grandmary paused for a moment. "First of all, Samantha," she said, "I think it is a mistake to assume that change means progress. The world got along quite well without all these new inventions and machines. Many of them have caused more confusion than they're worth."

Grandmary paused again. "Still," she said, "I think that the telephone has been of some help. Of course, it will never take the place of a courteous letter. But I think it does help Mrs. Hawkins when she orders meats and groceries. And it is a comfort if we should ever need the doctor or the fire department."

Samantha had something else she wanted to talk about. But once again she had to wait until Grandmary noticed and asked, "Is something bothering you, Samantha?"

"Grandmary, why isn't Edith Eddleton allowed to play with Nellie?" Samantha asked.

Grandmary looked surprised. "Why, Samantha," she said. "Edith is a young *lady.*"

Samantha thought that was ridiculous. But all she said was, "You let me play with Nellie."

"You are *helping* Nellie," said Grandmary, "not playing with her. There is a difference."

Samantha was quiet. She didn't like the difference.

Progress

CHAPTER 11

Samantha was delighted that Uncle Gard came to visit on Saturday. She was even more pleased to see that he had not brought his friend Cornelia with him. That meant that after tea with Grandmary, Samantha could have him all to herself.

The net was set up for lawn tennis. Samantha served the ball over the net. Uncle Gard dived for it and hit it back. Samantha swung her racquet and missed.

"Uncle Gard," Samantha called as she brought the ball back and moved closer to the net, "I need to know about progress. I need to know for the speaking contest. Two girls from Miss Crampton's can enter. The winner gets a gold medal. Oh, Uncle Gard, I really want to win. Can you help me?"

Uncle Gard whistled. "That's a pretty big order, Samantha. What do you need to know?"

"What's the best invention?" Samantha asked.

Her uncle thought a minute. "Well, electric lights are important, Sam. They make a big difference at night. And more and more people are getting them. I expect someday people will just have electric lights and we won't need gas lamps at all. And what about the automobile? Now, that's an important invention. People can go anywhere in automobiles."

"That's silly, Uncle Gard," said Samantha. "You can't go anywhere far away from a drugstore or you won't be able to get gasoline."

"Well, that's not a problem," said Uncle Gard. "Just take enough gasoline with you."

"And you can't go anywhere on a rainy day," said Samantha. "Automobiles get stuck in the mud."

"Have a heart, Sam," laughed Uncle Gard. "I thought you *liked* automobiles."

"I do," said Samantha as she got ready to hit the ball again. "But they're just not as much fun as horses."

"Why not?"

Samantha reached high and sent the ball sailing.

"You can't feed carrots to an automobile!"

For two weeks, Samantha worked hard to learn about progress in America. She read books about new inventions. She took notes about the ideas she got from talking to different people. Mrs. Hawkins said the best invention was the gas stove because it didn't get full of ashes like a coal stove, and you didn't have to keep coals hot all night and all summer. She said that was progress. And Hawkins told Samantha about factories. He said factories were the most important sign of progress in America because there was no end to what they could make. He said they made things fast and they made things cheap. And he said that meant there were more things for more people all over the country. That started Samantha thinking.

Every afternoon Samantha and Nellie had school in the tower room. Samantha wrote parts of her speech in her copybook and read them aloud to see how they sounded. Then she put the words a different way and read them aloud again. Nellie worked on reading, geography, and spelling. But she knew how much

Samantha wanted to win the speaking contest, and she tried not to disturb her.

One afternoon when Nellie was walking home with Samantha, they saw Edith Eddleton standing on the sidewalk with Clarisse Van Sicklen. "There's Samantha Parkington keeping company with the servants again," said Edith. She spoke very loudly. "Do you suppose she's practicing to be a wash-woman?"

Clarisse answered just as loudly, "Oh, no. I think Nellie is teaching her how to speak for the contest."

"Well, of course, that's it," said Edith. "Maybe we should all take lessons." And Edith and Clarisse snickered loudly.

Samantha ignored them and took Nellie's hand. But when they had walked on and could still hear the girls laughing behind them, Samantha said through clenched teeth, "Oh, Nellie, I wish girls were allowed to fight. I most surely do."

Later that afternoon, when Samantha and Nellie were working in Mount Better School, they needed more pencils. Samantha went downstairs to the library to get one from Grandmary's desk. On her way back she heard voices in the parlor. Even without looking at the calling cards on the hall table, Samantha knew who was visiting Grandmary. She recognized Mrs. Eddleton's high, shrill voice and Mrs. Ryland's rasping one. And she thought she heard Nellie's name.

Samantha moved closer to the door and peeked through a crack. Mrs. Eddleton was speaking. "Well, the entire neighborhood is simply shocked," she said.

Mrs. Ryland said, "Imagine bringing that whole ragged family to live right here, right in our neighborhood. I just don't know what got into Mrs. Van Sicklen."

"Actually, it was my idea," said Grandmary calmly as she poured the tea. "I urged Mrs. Van Sicklen to give them a home. Their life in the city was quite dreadful." She passed the tea to her guests. "I believe Mrs. Van Sicklen is quite pleased with them. They are all good workers."

The two visitors looked a little embarrassed, but Mrs. Eddleton continued, "My Edith says they are simply filthy, practically in rags."

"They are poor, of course," answered Grandmary. "But I have always found them as clean as any children, and surprisingly well mannered." Grandmary's back was very straight. Samantha recognized the frosty look in her eye that should have warned the visitors to be careful. But the visitors were too busy talking to notice.

Then Mrs. Ryland asked, "Do you really think it's wise to let Samantha spend so much time with them?"

"I believe Samantha is doing them a great deal of good," said Grandmary. "And it is our duty to do good where we can." She put her teacup down. "Would you care for more tea, ladies?" she asked in a voice that was more polite than friendly.

Samantha turned and hurried back up the hall. Suddenly she wanted to be close to Nellie.

After lunch on Thursday, all the girls in Miss Crampton's Academy filed quietly into the assembly room. They stood in front of their chairs until they had sung a hymn and said a prayer. Then they sat down with their backs straight and their hands folded in their laps. There was no whispering even before Miss Crampton began speaking.

"As you know, two girls from this Academy will represent all of us at the Speaking Contest tomorrow evening," Miss Crampton said. "Today, Miss Stevens and I will choose those two girls. They will be the girls who give the best speeches about progress in America."

Even with her hands folded, Samantha managed to cross her fingers. She took deep breaths to steady herself.

Miss Crampton continued. "I know that everyone in Miss Stevens's class has worked very hard on a speech. And I know we are all very eager to hear the results of this hard work. So I will say nothing more. Helen Whitney, will you please come forward?"

Helen walked up, curtsied, and gave her speech. Then each of the other girls in Samantha's class spoke. Some of their voices were shaky. Ida Dean spoke so softly, the audience could barely hear her. But she didn't faint.

At last Samantha's turn came. She was the last girl to speak. Her voice was clear and steady.

"American factories are the finest in the world," she began. "They are true signs of our progress. It used to take many hours to make a pair of shoes or a table by hand. Now machines can make hundreds of shoes and hundreds of tables in just a few hours. And they make thread and cloth, toys and bicycles, furniture, and even automobiles. These things cost less money than they used to because they are made by machines. So now more people can buy the things they want and the things they need. That is progress. Truly, we could not go forward into the twentieth century without our factories and without our machines. They are the greatest sign of progress in America."

There was applause in the room. Miss Stevens nodded in approval. Samantha beamed as she walked back to her seat.

Miss Crampton looked immensely pleased as she stepped to the front of the room. "All of our young ladies have done a splendid job," she said. "I am proud of each one of them. And now, it gives me great pleasure to announce our winners. Will Miss Samantha Parkington please step forward."

Samantha rose and walked to the front of the room again. Miss Crampton handed her an award. She felt her heart swell with pleasure as she heard the applause around her.

When the clapping stopped, Miss Crampton announced the other winner. It was Edith Eddleton.

Winners

CHAPTER 12

In Mount Better School that afternoon, Nellie watched proudly as Samantha pinned her award to the wall. "Can I hear your speech, Samantha?" Nellie asked. There was no doubt in Nellie's mind that her friend's speech would be the best ever written since Abraham Lincoln's.

Samantha cleared her throat and used her most proper voice. She repeated her speech just as she had at the Academy, remembering with a thrill the applause that had followed it. She finished proudly and then looked at Nellie for the praise she was sure would be coming.

But Nellie was staring at the floor and running her finger along the edge of the cushion.

"Well?" asked Samantha.

"It's very nice," said Nellie in a voice that said she didn't think it was nice at all.

Samantha felt hurt. "What's the matter with it?" she asked.

"It's very nice. It's just . . . well, it's just not very true," said Nellie.

"What do you mean?"

"I used to work in a factory, Samantha. It's not like that."

Nellie *had* worked in a factory. Samantha had almost forgotten that. "Well, what's a factory like, then?" she asked.

Nellie was quiet, as if she was remembering things she didn't want to remember. "I worked in a big room with other kids," she said finally. "Twenty others, I guess. But that didn't make it fun. We couldn't play. We couldn't even talk. The machines were too noisy. They were so noisy that when I got home at night my ears were buzzing and it was a long time before I could hear anything. We had to go to work at seven in the morning, and we worked until seven at night. Every day but Sunday."

Nellie continued, "I worked on the machines that

wound the thread. There were hundreds of spools. We had to put in new ones when the old ones got full, and we tied the thread if it broke. We had to stand up all the time. I got so tired, Samantha. My back hurt and my legs hurt and my arms got heavy. The machines got fuzz and dust all over everything. It was in the air, and it got in my mouth and made it hard to breathe."

Nellie was quiet again. Then she went on. "The room was awful hot in summer. But it was worse in winter because there wasn't any heat. Our feet nearly froze. We couldn't wear shoes."

Samantha was shocked. "You couldn't wear shoes?" she asked.

"We had to climb on the machines to change the spools, and shoes could make us slip. The machines were so strong, they could break your hand or your foot or pull a finger off as easy as anything. We all had to have our hair short. If your hair was long, the machines could catch it and pull it right out. They just kept winding. Once I saw that happen to a girl. She was just standing there, and then suddenly she was screaming and half her head was bleeding. She almost died."

Nellie was running her finger along the edge of the cushion again. "They paid us one dollar and eighty cents a week." She looked straight at her friend. "That's why thread is so cheap."

Samantha stared at Nellie. She couldn't move. She felt numb and cold, but her scalp was tingling and her arms had a strange ache in them.

The Mount Bedford Opera House was used for most of the town's special events. It served Mount Bedford for everything from roller-skating parties to concerts. On the evening of the Young People's Speaking Contest it was filled with wooden chairs.

The contest speakers sat on the stage, facing parents and friends from all over town. Grandmary sat in the second row, wearing a gray silk dress and looking calm and stately. Nellie sat with her mother near the back of the room. She looked shy and out of place.

As the president of the Mount Bedford Ladies Club stepped to the front of the stage, smiling and bobbing her head, the room grew quiet. She welcomed everyone, introduced the speakers, and told what schools they represented. Then it was time for the speeches.

One of the boys from Lessing's School told about a new building that was twenty stories high. He said that from now on, all cities would be different because of it. Another boy talked about automobiles, and someone spoke about electric lights. A girl from the public school talked about medicine. She said people didn't get sick as much as they used to. Then it was Edith Eddleton's turn.

Edith walked to the front of the stage like an army general. She paused for a moment with her head a little to one side. Then she boomed out her speech in a voice meant to reach the Opera House doors and beyond.

"We are indeed fortunate to live in this age of progress. Progress is the great American adventure. In the old days, a man had to work all day and all night to support himself and his family. But now, in modern America, great machines can be a great benefit to everyone. Now everyone can have all he needs without a difficult struggle. Fortunes can be made now as never before. Now, with the help of machines, anyone can become wealthy. What a great opportunity man has in the twentieth century. Are we not fortunate to live in this great age of progress?"

Everyone clapped loudly as Edith returned to her chair in triumph. She sat down, smoothed her dress, and smiled at Samantha.

Then Samantha heard her name called. She walked to the front of the stage calmly. She didn't look at Miss Crampton and Miss Stevens. She knew what they were expecting her to say.

Samantha stood tall and looked straight ahead. In her mind she could hear the words she had been practicing ever since her last lesson in Mount Better School.

"Americans are very proud of being modern," Samantha began. "We are proud of our progress. We are proud of the machines in our factories because they make so many new things for us. But Americans are proud of being truthful, too. If we were truthful, we would say that the factory machines make things fast and cheap, but they are dangerous, too. They can hurt the children who work in the factories. The machines can break their arms. They can cut off their fingers.

They can make children sick. And children who work in factories don't have time to play or go to school. They are too tired." Samantha spoke calmly and clearly. She had discovered something. She had discovered that it is easy to talk to people, even to many people, if you really believe what you are saying.

"If our factories can hurt children, then we have not made good progress in America," Samantha continued. "And I believe Americans want to be good. I believe we want to be kind. And if we are kind, I believe we will take care of the children. Then we can truly be proud of our factories and our progress."

As Samantha walked back to her chair at the end of her speech, there was a long silence. Grandmary looked a little shocked. How could Samantha have known about such things? Then Grandmary looked back at Nellie. Nellie was sitting with her back straight and her eyes shining. And Grandmary understood. A proud smile spread across her face and she began to applaud. Her applause joined the clapping that began all over the room and grew into a long, loud roar of approval.

Edith Eddleton looked rather like a snowman that had been left too long in the sun.

The next time Samantha and Nellie sat in Mount Better School, it was not for a lesson. It was for a celebration. Samantha's first-prize medal hung from its blue ribbon on the schoolroom wall.

The girls were eating cookies and little cakes with pink frosting. Mrs. Hawkins had made them a whole pitcher of lemonade. They sat on cushions, with napkins spread on their laps, feeling very pleased with themselves.

Nellie sighed happily as she finished a cookie. She leaned back against the wall. "I'm glad we're celebrating today, Samantha. Something nice happened to me, too."

"Oh?" said Samantha, eager to share her friend's good news. "What?"

Nellie smiled shyly. "I moved to third grade."

Samantha jumped up, spun around, and clapped her hands. "Nellie, that's wonderful! That's just wonderful!" Then she stopped and looked at her friend.

Nellie didn't look as happy as she should. "You didn't tell me right away, Nellie. What's wrong?" asked Samantha.

Nellie looked down at her napkin. Then she looked back at Samantha. "I have the desk next to Eddie Ryland."

Samantha's eyes grew wide and she sank back to the floor. "Ooohh, Nellie," she said with feeling. Both girls were quiet for a minute. Then Samantha pushed the cookies away and reached for a book. "Hurry up and finish your lemonade. We've got to start studying. You've got to move up to the head of the class!"

Christmas Wishes

CHAPTER 13

amantha loved walking home from school in December. All of Mount Bedford seemed to be decorated for Christmas. The tree branches sparkled with silvery snowflakes. Green wreaths with sprigs of red holly hung on front doors and in shop windows. Shoppers bustled about wearing colorful coats and bright smiles. *Everything's so cheerful,* Samantha thought as she turned onto High Street. *And on Saturday, Nellie and I are going to finish making decorations for the house. Grandmary will be so surprised!*

Samantha was surprised to hear someone call her name. "Wait, Samantha!" It was Samantha's friend Ida, who rushed across the street and pressed a red envelope into Samantha's hand. "I want to give you this," Ida said with excitement.

Samantha pulled off her mittens, tore open the flap, and drew out a card shaped like a Christmas stocking and edged with paper lace. It said:

Miss Ida Dean requests
the pleasure of your company
at a Christmas Party
to be held at
six o'clock in the evening
Thursday, December 22
R.S.V.P.

"Ooh, Ida," Samantha squealed. Her breath made little clouds in the chilly air.

"I hope you can come," Ida said. "My brother is going to do magic tricks, and we'll play ladies' ring and charades!"

"Oh, it sounds wonderful!" Samantha said. "Ida, I think this is going to be the best Christmas ever!"

"Me, too," Ida agreed. "Especially if I get a new pair

of ice skates. But do you know what I really want?"

"A dollhouse?" Samantha guessed.

"No."

"A sled?"

"No."

"A stereoscope?"

"No. A dog," Ida said. "A real cocker spaniel puppy!"

"Puppies are so cute! Do you think you'll get one?" Samantha asked.

"I don't know. I've asked and asked, though," Ida replied. "What are you hoping for?"

Samantha sighed. "What I really want is the doll I saw at Schofield's Toy Store," she said. "I want that doll more than anything in the world!"

"What's she like?" Ida wondered.

"She's beautiful," Samantha replied. "She's dressed all in pink, even her shoes, and in her hand there's a tiny little—"

"Let's go look!" Ida interrupted.

The two girls raced down the street. As they ran, snowflakes swirled around them, clinging to their knitted mittens, resting in their hair, and brushing their cheeks like small, quick kisses.

At Schofield's Toy Store, the girls pressed their noses to the cold glass window. "There she is!" Samantha breathed. She pointed to a group of dolls that seemed to be dancing. They twirled around a doll who wore a lacy pink dress, pink pantalettes, and pink slippers. The doll held a tiny wooden soldier that looked just like the Nutcracker in the ballet.

"I love that Nutcracker doll," Samantha said.

"Well, do you think your grandmother will give it to you?" Ida asked.

"No . . ." Samantha answered slowly, looking down at her wet black boots. "I don't think so. I haven't asked her."

"You haven't *asked*?" Ida was puzzled. "Why not?"

"I just can't."

"What do you mean you *can't*?" Ida's voice rose. "Why can't you?"

"Because of Lydia," Samantha replied.

"You mean because you gave Lydia away?" Ida asked.

Samantha nodded.

"I would never, ever give a doll away. Especially a doll my grandmother had given to me!" Ida declared.

"But I gave Lydia to Nellie because she had never

owned a doll in her life—not ever!"

"Oh." Ida paused. Then she added, "Well, now *you* don't have a doll. So why don't you ask your grandmother for this one?"

Samantha took one last look at the doll in the window, then shook her head. "I just don't think Grandmary would buy me another doll so soon. She would probably think it was a terrible extravagance."

"But you should ask her anyway," Ida insisted as they walked toward Chestnut Street. "After all, the worst she can say is no."

"Maybe. Maybe I could ask her," Samantha said, more to herself than to Ida. They'd reached the corner, and Ida raced off into the snowflakes.

"Good-bye, Samantha," she called.

"See you tomorrow!" Samantha shouted back. She dodged a coal wagon, then ran up Chestnut Street to Grandmary's house.

Samantha let herself in the big front door and was immediately welcomed by the sweet, warm smell of just-baked sugar cookies. She followed the delicious scent to the kitchen. There was Mrs. Hawkins, stirring a pitcher of hot cocoa.

"Heavens, child! You're a sorry sight. Come, take off those cold, wet things." Mrs. Hawkins helped Samantha out of her wet coat and snow-caked boots, then sat her by the warm oven. "There, that's better," Mrs. Hawkins cooed, bringing Samantha the plate of sugar cookies. "Get good and warm now. Here, I've made your hot cocoa just the way you like it—with lots of cinnamon."

Samantha ate a sugar cookie and took sips of the cocoa. When she felt warm inside and out, she said, "Mrs. Hawkins, Christmas is only two weeks away."

"That it is, Samantha, and it seems I'll never get everything done."

Samantha reached into her pocket and took out a folded piece of paper. She smoothed it open and said, "Look! I've made a design we can use for the gingerbread house."

Mrs. Hawkins squinted at the paper. "Oh, where did I put my spectacles?" she asked, searching around the table.

Samantha handed Mrs. Hawkins her glasses, which had been lying on top of the breadbox.

"Thanks, love. I seem to be forever looking for

them," Mrs. Hawkins said, setting them on her nose. "Now, let's see." She studied the drawing silently for a few moments, then remarked, "It's cleverly planned, Samantha, but how *big* are you expecting this gingerbread house to be?"

"About two feet across and two feet high."

"Two feet high! And you're sure this isn't a gingerbread train station?" Mrs. Hawkins teased.

"It *is* rather big," Samantha admitted, "but it's got to hold up a lot of things. We'll use taffy sticks for pillars and caramel squares for the doors. Cinnamon drops make the best chimney bricks, and for the drawbridge we can use licorice ropes!"

"My!" Mrs. Hawkins said. "It sounds fancy."

"But we can do it—I know we can. Don't you think so, Mrs. Hawkins?" Samantha asked.

Mrs. Hawkins looked over the drawing again. "Yes, Samantha, I do believe that with a lot of ingredients, and quite a bit of time, and just a pinch of luck, we can make this house."

"Oh, I knew you'd say yes, Mrs. Hawkins. Thank you so much!" Samantha cried, jumping up and giving her a hug. "Let's do it Saturday!"

Presents and a Party Dress

CHAPTER 14

Samantha went up to her bedroom, closed the door, and turned the big brass key to lock it. Then she pulled her chair into the closet and climbed up on it. From the top of the chair she could just reach the big pink hatbox on the highest shelf. She brought it down and set it carefully on her bed.

The hatbox was Samantha's Christmas box. It held all the presents she was making. She unpacked them now, one by one.

First she lifted out the satin pincushion she'd made for Jessie. It was shaped like a strawberry and stuffed with a cup of sawdust from the butcher shop.

Next Samantha took out a book about a lost dog. It was for Nathaniel, Jessie's baby. Samantha had written it herself and stitched it together with red yarn.

Grandmary's gift was underneath the book. It was a heart made from lace and stuffed with dried rose petals. Samantha sniffed it. She knew Grandmary would put it with her handkerchiefs to make them smell pretty.

Mrs. Hawkins's gift was a chain to attach to her glasses so she'd never lose them again. And for Nellie, Samantha had made a blue velvet cape for Lydia to wear. Samantha held the cape and thought about how beautiful Lydia would look in it.

At last Samantha reached her favorite gift of all. It was for Uncle Gard. Uncle Gard's present wasn't finished yet, but already it was more beautiful than anything Samantha had ever made. It was a box—a small box, just the right size for cuff links. Samantha had decorated it with pictures of animals, leaves, berries, fruits, and flowers from her collection of paper scraps. She had carefully cut out each piece of scrap. Then she'd glued them, one by one, to the sides of the box.

Now only the lid was left to be decorated. Samantha sat on the floor with her pot of glue and her collection of scraps spread around her. Very, very carefully she brushed the back of a purple pansy with glue and held it firmly on the box. After the glue had dried, she picked up one last picture—her favorite one. It was a heart with the words "with love" written on it. Samantha placed it in the very center of the lid. It was perfect. She *knew* Uncle Gard would like this present best of any he would get on Christmas morning.

Just then someone knocked at her door.

"Miss Samantha."

"Just a minute, Jessie!" Samantha called. Quickly, she stuffed her presents back into the hatbox and pushed it under her bed.

"Open the door, child!"

Samantha hid her scrap collection next to the hat-box, scooted the chair out of her closet, and hurried to unlock her bedroom door.

"Come along, now. I've finished your Christmas dress. We just need to hem it," the seamstress said. Samantha followed her upstairs into the little sewing room. She could hardly wait to see the new party dress Jessie had made.

"Where is it?" Samantha asked, looking around the room.

"Oh, you'll see it in good time," Jessie said, smiling slyly. "Now, take off that dress, close your eyes, and raise your arms."

Samantha did as she was told and felt something crisp and cool slide over her head.

"Heavens!" Jessie gasped.

"What's the matter?" Samantha asked, keeping her eyes closed.

"Why, you've grown two inches since I measured you. Miss Samantha, you shoot up faster than smoke in a chimney!"

"May I open my eyes now, Jessie?"

"Not just yet. First let me fix the hem. That'll make a big difference."

Samantha waited patiently with her eyes still closed. "Jessie?"

"Mmmmm?" Jessie's mouth was full of pins.

"Ida Dean is having a Christmas party in two weeks. Do you think I can wear this dress?"

Jessie pulled the last pins out of her mouth. "I don't know, child. You'll have to ask your grandmother."

"Jessie . . . ?" Samantha started up again.

"Yes, Miss Samantha?"

"I just love Christmas. I love everything about it. Even getting ready for Christmas is fun."

"I'm sure it is," Jessie laughed.

"I've made all the decorations for the house already," Samantha added. "I've got paper snowflakes and cotton snowmen and things for the tree. And on Saturday morning, Nellie is coming over to help me make pinecone wreaths."

"Did you make the angels out of that blue silk I gave you?" Jessie asked.

"I made ten of them, just the way you showed me!"

"You *have* been working hard!" Jessie said.

"Now can I see myself, Jessie?" Samantha asked eagerly.

"Yes, it's all done."

Samantha opened her eyes and faced the long mirror. Slowly, she turned herself around. The red taffeta dress shimmered and made ever-so-soft swishing sounds as Samantha moved. It was the color of ripe cranberries. A snowy white lace collar circled the neck, and a crisp white sash wrapped her hips and tied in a bow in front.

"Oh, Jessie, this is the most gorgeous dress in the

whole world," Samantha pronounced solemnly.

"I agree with you there, Miss Samantha! It's a dress fine enough for a princess, if I do say so myself!"

Samantha heard someone sniff. Elsa was standing at the door scowling. "Playing dress-up at this hour!" she snipped. "It's all very well to fuss with them frills, but not at teatime. Your grandmother told me to fetch you, and here you are not even properly dressed!"

"Now, Elsa, Miss Samantha will be right down," Jessie answered.

"Fussing with frills at teatime!" Elsa muttered to herself as she turned. Her shoes scolded *tsk tsk tsk* as she walked down the hall.

Jessie helped Samantha out of the new dress and back into her regular clothes. Samantha straightened her stockings and raced downstairs.

"Grandmary, Grandmary!" she burst out. She remembered to make a curtsy. "I have the most exciting news!"

"How delightful," replied Grandmary as she lifted the teapot. "Come, let's have our tea."

Just as Samantha was sure she couldn't wait a moment longer, her grandmother asked, "And what is your news, Samantha?"

"My friend Ida Dean is having a Christmas party. It's a week from Thursday, and it's at night! Her brother will do magic tricks and we're going to play games, and it will be the most wonderful party of all. May I go? And may I wear my new Christmas dress?"

Grandmary took a sip of tea. "Samantha dear, you really must learn to ask only *one* question at a time. *Two* questions at once are quite . . . unbalancing. Now, as to the first question—of course you may go, my dear. And as to the second question—yes, you may wear your new dress. You grow so fast, you might as well get all the wear you can out of it."

"Thank you, Grandmary," Samantha said happily. "I'll have the best time."

"And now I have a surprise for you," Grandmary announced.

There was a long pause as Grandmary buttered a biscuit. She was not one to hurry surprises. Finally she said, "As you know, Samantha, your Uncle Gardner will spend Christmas with us as he always has. But this year he is not coming alone. He is bringing Miss Cornelia Pitt with him. She will celebrate the holidays here in Mount Bedford and stay on until the New Year."

Miss Cornelia Pitt? Grandmary meant Cornelia! Samantha thought of Uncle Gard's friend, who lived in New York. Cornelia was beautiful and so elegant. Her clothes were the latest style, and she always smelled of violets.

"Remember, Samantha," Grandmary continued, "Cornelia is a special friend of your uncle's. We must make her feel welcome."

"Oh, I'll welcome her," Samantha said. "And I'll make this the best Christmas *she's* ever had, too. That will be easy. I've already made all the decorations and planned the gingerbread house."

"That's very good of you, Samantha," Grandmary said. "But perhaps you have done enough already. Everyone in the house will be very busy now, and it may be best if you just stay out of the way."

Samantha wondered why grown-ups always thought the most helpful thing she could do was nothing at all. Didn't they understand what still had to be done? Someone had to string cranberries and hang snowflakes on the windows. Someone had to pick out just the right candy for the gingerbread house. Someone had to help Uncle Gard find a perfect Christmas tree. Samantha could do all those things. And now that Cornelia was coming, she had more to do. She would have to get one more present—something very nice and very elegant for Cornelia. But what?

"It's so *hard* to figure out gifts!" Samantha found herself saying aloud.

"What is that you said, dear?" Grandmary asked.

"I was just thinking, Grandmary, how hard it is to know what somebody might want for Christmas. I mean, most of the time you just have to guess!"

Grandmary smiled. "You're entirely correct, Samantha. Of course, sometimes a person might let you know what may be appropriate."

"Yes, Grandmary," Samantha said, remembering her own secret wish for Christmas. She thought of what Ida had said, and the words floated back to her. *You should ask her anyway,* they whispered. *The worst she can say is no.*

"Grandmary," Samantha said, clearing her throat.

"Yes, Samantha?" her grandmother answered, not looking up as she poured more tea.

"Grandmary, I wanted to ask if . . . if . . ."

"Yes?" Now Grandmary seemed to stare right through Samantha.

"Grandmary, I just wanted to ask you if . . . well . . ."

"Samantha dear, speak up. I can hardly hear you when you mumble!"

"Grandmary, I wanted to tell you that . . ."

"Come to the point, Samantha."

". . . that I think it's going to snow through the weekend!" Samantha blurted out, red-faced and shy.

"Yes, dear, I quite agree with you."

It was no use. Samantha knew she couldn't ask Grandmary for the doll. She didn't have the courage.

Decorations and Disappointments

CHAPTER 15

On Saturday morning, when their pinecone wreaths were made, Samantha showed Nellie some of the presents in her pink hatbox. She saved Uncle Gard's box until last. "And this is the best present of all," she said proudly as she handed it to Nellie.

"Oh, it really is," Nellie agreed. "I know your uncle will like it."

"He'll *love* it," Samantha insisted. "He'll know it's the nicest thing I've ever made for anyone."

"What are you giving your grandmother?" Nellie asked.

Samantha showed her the sweet-smelling sachet she had made. "Grandmary says homemade gifts are the best ones because you give of yourself when you make them. But I'll have to buy Cornelia's present.

There's not enough time to make something really special for her," Samantha said. "I wish I knew what to get."

"What about bath salts?" Nellie suggested. "Mrs. Van Sicklen has some in a tall bottle with a fancy glass top."

"Yes, bath salts are nice," Samantha agreed. Then she shook her head. "But I don't think bath salts are nice enough for Cornelia."

"How about hankies?" Nellie asked.

"Well, maybe if they had lace edges," Samantha said hopefully. Then she thought of Cornelia riding in Uncle Gard's automobile, and even hankies with lace edges seemed like a dull sort of present. "No, Nellie, I need to think of something *really* special."

"Perfume?" Nellie suggested.

"That would be special enough, but I don't think I have enough money for perfume." Samantha sighed. "Well, I can go talk to Jessie later. Maybe she'll know what I should get for Cornelia."

"I'm giving Mrs. Van Sicklen my biggest pinecone wreath," Nellie said. She looked proudly at the wreaths she'd lined up on the floor of Samantha's room. "Do you think she'll like it?"

"Of course she will," Samantha assured her friend. "Everyone loves Christmas decorations." She reached under her bed, pulled out a cardboard box with DECORATIONS written on all four sides, and took out the cotton snowmen, silk angels, and paper snowflakes she'd been making since Thanksgiving. "Look what I'm putting up this afternoon," she said.

"Samantha, your house is going to look like a fairy-land," Nellie exclaimed.

"Especially with these snowflakes," Samantha agreed.

Later that afternoon, after Nellie had gone home, Samantha lugged her decoration box down the long, winding staircase. *I'll trim the banister first,* she thought. At the bottom of the stairs, she unpacked a long string of cranberries. She was about to wind it around the polished railing when a strange voice stopped her.

"Excuse me, young lady," said a tall, red-haired man. He wore a navy blue uniform almost like a soldier's. The words *Farrola Florist* were on the pocket.

The man set down a large box that held spicy-scented pine garlands with enormous red bows. He drew a garland out slowly, handling it as delicately as if it were a snake. "Now if you would just step out of the way, miss," he continued as he began to wrap the garland gracefully around the banister.

"I have some decorations, too," Samantha told the man. "I have a cranberry garland. Well, I guess you'd call it a string of cranberries. It would look quite nice together with—"

"Please, miss," the red-haired man sighed, "if you could just stand back and try not to disturb the garland. It's a bit fragile."

Samantha stepped back and found herself standing on Hawkins's toes.

"Oh, Hawkins, I'm so sorry," she said.

"That's quite all right, Miss Samantha. Now, if you'll excuse me . . ."

Hawkins was carrying another box marked *Farrola Florist* into the parlor. Two more large boxes were already on the rug.

"What's in all these boxes?" asked Samantha.

"Holiday adornments," he said. "Christmas decorations." Samantha saw holly and laurel wreaths and bouquets of Christmas roses—red ones, of course.

She counted four ropes of ivy, eight hoops of mistletoe, and two miniature trees. One was trimmed with little crab apples and one was full of tiny oranges. "Your grandmother wishes the house to be in full Yuletide splendor for Miss Cornelia's visit," Hawkins explained. He turned to drape an ivy rope across the fireplace mantel.

Samantha could not believe what she was seeing. "But Hawkins, I've already *made* decorations, lots of them, enough for the whole house!"

Hawkins was struggling so hard with the ivy that he didn't seem to hear.

Samantha picked up her box of decorations and walked into the dining room. No one was around, so she took out her fuzzy snowmen first. She hung six of them from the wall lamps, using green ribbon. Two more were soon propped up beside the huge meat platter on the china cabinet. Four snowmen stood together around a pile of pinecones in the center of the table.

Using the tiniest drops of glue, Samantha stuck paper snowflakes to the dining room windows. She took down a small oil painting and in its place hung her largest pinecone wreath. The cranberry garland went across the dining room curtains.

When Samantha had finished, she sat down to admire her work. The whole room was like a tiny indoor forest filled with pinecones and red berries. Cotton snowmen peeked out from the dark furniture as if they were hiding behind tall trees. Paper snowflakes seemed to float on the windows. *It's beautiful,* Samantha thought. *It's like a winter wonderland—and I did it all by myself.*

Someone gasped. "Sakes alive! What is this nonsense?"

It was Elsa.

The maid went straight to the windows and began tearing off Samantha's snowflakes. "It's not as if a body didn't have enough to do, what with the washing and dusting and polishing," Elsa muttered. "And now having to put up with all this holiday hoopla. Whatever made the child set all them dustcatchers around?"

Samantha jumped out of her chair. "They're not dustcatchers! They're snowflakes and cranberry garlands and snowmen and . . . and . . . and I made them!"

Elsa was speechless for a moment. Then she said firmly, "Mr. Hawkins and a young florist gentleman are decorating the house just as your grandmother wished—fine and fancy for Miss Cornelia's visit. So it's no use trying to tell me about your snowmice!"

"Snow*men*," Samantha sniffed, scooping up the decorations that Elsa had piled on the floor.

"Whatever," Elsa huffed. "Run along now. I've got the devil's own work dusting this chandelier. Miss Cornelia will be here for Christmas dinner, and it's got to sparkle."

"You'd think it was Cornelia Day, not Christmas Day," Samantha grumbled, almost loud enough for Elsa to hear. She went to the kitchen. Maybe a visit with Mrs. Hawkins would cheer her up.

The kitchen was perfumed with delicious smells. Two mince pies and a pound cake had just come out of the oven. There were homemade peppermint drops cooling on the table. At the sink, Mrs. Hawkins was pouring quince jam into glass jars. Her face was as red as the cranberry sauce that bubbled on the stove.

Samantha sat down at the table and popped one of the peppermint drops into her mouth. "You know,

Mrs. Hawkins," she said, "I just thought of an idea."

There was no answer.

"Mrs. Hawkins?"

"Yes, dear," Mrs. Hawkins replied, not looking up from her jam.

"I said that I just thought of something."

"Hmmm, what's that?"

"Well, we could cover the walls of the gingerbread house with peppermint drops and it would look like a magic candy house—like the candy house in *Hansel and Gretel.*"

"Samantha," Mrs. Hawkins said with a sigh, "I know you'll be disappointed, but I don't see that we can make a gingerbread house after all. With your Uncle Gard's friend coming and your grandmother wanting everything so special for her, there's a tremendous lot of cooking to be done. There's just no time for a gingerbread house this year."

"Not *any* gingerbread house?" Samantha asked with disbelief. "Not even a little one?"

"Not even a little one, Samantha. Truly I'm sorry, but I think you're old enough to understand."

"Yes, I understand," said Samantha sadly. "I really

do, Mrs. Hawkins." She left the kitchen mumbling, "I understand that if Cornelia weren't coming, everything would be fine."

She picked up her box of decorations and hauled it up the stairway. The corner of the box bumped the garland on the banister and knocked a bow crooked. Samantha didn't straighten it.

In her room, Samantha unpacked her decorations again. *I'll put them up here,* she said to herself. *If everyone else thinks snowflakes are a bother, then they can stay out of my room.* She noticed that two of her best snowflakes had been ruined and decided to make new ones. She went to her desk to hunt for a pair of scissors.

Why is everyone making such a fuss over Cornelia? Samantha asked herself as she folded a piece of tissue paper. *There's nothing special about her. Nothing special at all. I don't know why I even bothered to worry about her present. I'll just give her hankies for Christmas. Plain, boring, lie-in-the-box hankies!*

There was a knock at Samantha's door. She opened it to find Grandmary standing there.

"Samantha dear, your Uncle Gardner has just

telephoned to say that he and Cornelia will arrive late Thursday afternoon. We must welcome Cornelia properly, so I am afraid that going to a party that evening is out of the question. You will need to send Ida Dean your regrets."

"Oh, Grandmary, no!" Samantha cried.

"It is the polite thing to do, Samantha," Grandmary said kindly but firmly.

Stupid Cornelia is ruining Christmas, Samantha thought. *She's ruining it for everybody, but mostly she's ruining it for me.*

"I hate Cornelia!" Samantha said when she was sure Grandmary couldn't hear her. Slowly, hot tears began to roll down her cheeks.

"I'm glad I don't have enough money to buy her perfume. I won't buy her handkerchiefs, either. I wouldn't give Cornelia bath salts in a paper bag. In fact, I won't give her anything at all for Christmas." The tears came faster, and Samantha began to sob.

Someone Very Special

CHAPTER 16

Your house looks especially lovely with all the Christmas decorations," Cornelia said. Sunlight poured through the parlor windows and danced in her soft, wavy hair.

"Thank you," Grandmary answered. "We did want things to be festive for you."

Samantha didn't say anything. She didn't even look at Cornelia.

"I hope the trip down wasn't too tiring for you," said Grandmary as she passed a plate of tiny tea sandwiches.

"Oh, no," Cornelia replied. "I do love motorcars, and Gard—I mean Gardner—is such a good driver."

Grandmary smiled. "You are certainly brave, my dear, to ride in those new machines."

"I love travel of any kind," Cornelia responded,

her brown eyes sparkling. "When the new flying machines begin to carry passengers, I plan to ride in one of them, too."

So do I! Samantha thought. *I'd love to see Mount Bedford the way a bird sees it!*

Grandmary raised her eyebrows. "Well," she said to Cornelia, "I don't think there will ever be much chance of ladies traveling in airplanes!"

"I'm not so sure," Cornelia said gently, surprising Samantha with how gracefully she could disagree with Grandmary. "I've read in the newspaper that travel by airplane might be possible one day, even across the ocean."

Samantha looked at Grandmary. She knew her grandmother thought this was nonsense. But Grandmary merely replied, "Perhaps."

Uncle Gard laughed. "By Jupiter, any sort of travel is fine with me! Let them put me in a hot air balloon or in a rickshaw or on an elephant. I'd even let them shoot me out of a cannon!"

"Gardner!" Grandmary exclaimed. She pretended to be shocked, and Samantha giggled.

"Of course I think the *best* form of travel is

sledding," Uncle Gard added. He turned to Samantha. "Don't you, Sam?"

"Oh, yes," Samantha agreed, "only I haven't gone yet this winter."

"Well, why don't we go sledding tomorrow morning?" suggested Cornelia.

"Do you really think . . . ?" Grandmary began.

Cornelia's large brown eyes were soft and earnest. "It's such good, wholesome exercise," she said.

"Please, Grandmary," Samantha pleaded. "I *love* sledding!"

"All right." Grandmary smiled. "Sledding tomorrow morning will be fine."

"Hurrah!" cried Samantha. Right then she made up her mind to give Cornelia something nice for Christmas after all. Maybe bath salts. The kind in the tall bottle with the fancy glass top.

The sun sparkled on Fairwind Hill the next morning. The sky was deep blue and cloudless, the air was clean and cool, and all of Mount Bedford lay below, tucked under a soft, thick blanket of snow.

"I love this hill," Uncle Gard said as they pulled the sled to the top. "When I was a boy, I'd come up here to imagine I was in heaven."

Cornelia smiled. "Gard, I think you could imagine *anything* if you tried."

"I couldn't imagine life without you," Gard murmured.

Samantha caught his words. *Uncle Gard is in love!* she said to herself. *He loves Cornelia!*

"Sam," Uncle Gard called over his shoulder, "who's going to steer?"

"You steer the sled, Uncle Gard. I want to be in the middle."

"All right," Uncle Gard laughed. "Let's go!"

The three piled on the sled. Uncle Gard sat in front, then Samantha, and behind them both, Cornelia.

"I feel somewhat like a caboose," Cornelia said, making Samantha laugh.

"Hold on!" Uncle Gard called. With a tremendous whoosh they were gone, skimming down the hillside at top speed.

"Ooooh!" cried Samantha with delight.

"Hurrah!" came Cornelia's unladylike shout.

The sled slid faster and faster, skidding and hopping down the hill. "Watch out!" Uncle Gard yelled.

But it was too late.

The sled veered out of control, narrowly missed a tree, and tipped over. The passengers spilled out into the snow.

"Oof!" Samantha grunted, wiping the soft powder from her face.

Uncle Gard was in front of her, laughing and pointing back up the hill. Samantha turned to see what he thought was so funny. It was Cornelia! She had landed on her stomach, and her hat had flown right off her head. She looked most unladylike with her legs tangled, her face red as a beet, and her beautiful hair all stringy and wet. But she was laughing, too! Samantha had never seen anything like it—a grown-up lady who knew how to play. *Cornelia is fun! I see why Uncle Gard loves her,* Samantha thought.

"Come on!" Cornelia cried, pulling herself up and dusting off the snow. "Let's do it again!"

And they did. They sledded until they were so out of breath, their clothes so wet, and their noses so red that they could do nothing but hurry home to a hot lunch with Grandmary.

After lunch they decided to go shopping. They piled into Uncle Gard's automobile, and with a loud *ooh-wah ooh-wah* from the horn, they rumbled off toward High Street.

This year the stores seemed more beautiful than ever. Miss Smith's Stationery Shop had a revolving Christmas tree made of Christmas cards. As a music box played "Joy to the World," the tree turned round and round.

Mr. Jerome, the shoemaker, had four mechanical elves in his window. They hammered, stitched, and polished tiny shoes. Their mouths opened and closed as they worked, and their pointy-hatted heads turned from side to side.

"Aren't they cute?" Samantha asked. She had seen the elves every Christmas she could remember, yet each year they delighted her as if she had never seen them before.

"Yes, I love the store windows at Christmastime, too," Cornelia replied enthusiastically.

Next they came to Mr. Carruthers's Candy Shop.

Samantha thought Mr. Carruthers's shop was always a wonderful place, but now she thought it was spectacular. Large red bins shaped like sleighs were heaped with sweets.

"Oh, don't those look delicious?" Cornelia pointed to the mounds of light and dark chocolates on a small silver tray inside a glass case. "I just love chocolate truffles," she said.

"Well, these are the finest in Mount Bedford," Mr. Carruthers informed her. "Jolie Chocolates. They arrived just this week from France."

"They do look special," Uncle Gard remarked, "although I prefer jelly beans myself."

Samantha had paused in front of some colored sugar wafers. "Oh, Samantha, wouldn't these be perfect on a gingerbread house?" Cornelia asked her. "When I was a girl, I always decorated a gingerbread house."

"I always decorated a gingerbread house, too," Samantha said. "This year Mrs. Hawkins doesn't have time to help me, though."

"Then why don't you and I make a gingerbread house?" Cornelia asked. "We could do it tomorrow morning."

"Oh, I'd like that. I'd like that very much!" Samantha said. They picked out all the trimmings right then. Mr. Carruthers filled several paper bags with lemon drops, sugar wafers, jelly beans, and honey sticks.

Cornelia is really too nice for bath salts, Samantha thought as they walked out of the store. *She deserves something special. Maybe I'll get her handkerchiefs. Linen handkerchiefs with lace edges.*

When they crossed Felter Street, Samantha heard the tinkly music of toy pianos. "Let's go to Schofield's Toy Store!" she cried.

The store was crowded, but Uncle Gard, Cornelia, and Samantha managed to make their way inside. Uncle Gard led Cornelia to the back of the shop to look at the toy soldiers, and Samantha went straight to the window to look at the dolls. When she saw that the lovely Nutcracker doll was still there, her heart sank. She'd hoped it would be gone because Grandmary had bought it for her, but she knew that was a foolish hope. Grandmary didn't even know that Samantha wanted this doll more than anything in the world. Grandmary *couldn't* know that because

Samantha hadn't told her. And now Samantha was sure that someone else would buy the doll for some other girl—maybe for one of the girls in the store right this minute.

Just then a hand reached into the display and picked up the beautiful Nutcracker doll. "Oh, look at this doll! Isn't she exquisite?"

Samantha was startled. She hadn't heard anyone come up behind her. She turned to find Cornelia.

"And look at the tiny Nutcracker in her arms," Cornelia exclaimed. "This is the most wonderful doll in the store. Don't you think so, Samantha?"

"Oh, yes," Samantha agreed out loud. To herself she said, *Cornelia understands. She knows what's special.* And for just a moment, she forgot to be sad about the doll she would never have.

Just then Uncle Gard returned. "The toy soldiers said we'd better march. Grandmary will worry if we're late."

They pushed their way out of the busy store, but when they reached the car, Samantha announced, "I won't be coming home with you."

"What do you mean?" Uncle Gard asked.

"I—I forgot something. I forgot to—to buy the vanilla Mrs. Hawkins asked me to pick up for her," Samantha lied. "I'll get it and walk home."

"Nonsense, Sam," Uncle Gard said. "We'll go together."

"No—no, really," Samantha said, "I would rather go alone and walk. I love the streets at Christmastime."

Uncle Gard was about to say no again, but something in Samantha's voice must have told him this was important. After a pause he said, "All right, Sam, go if you want. But don't be late!"

When she was sure the automobile had turned the corner, Samantha ran back up High Street to Mr. Carruthers's Candy Shop. The little bell over the door tinkled as she went inside.

"Well, young lady," Mr. Carruthers said, "how can I help you this time?"

"A pound of Jolie French chocolates, please."

"A whole pound?" Mr. Carruthers asked, his white eyebrows twitching up with surprise.

"A whole pound," Samantha repeated.

"This must be for someone really special."

"Oh, yes, Mr. Carruthers—someone *very* special."

A Guessing Game

CHAPTER 17

On Christmas Eve morning, Samantha and Cornelia put the finishing touches on their gingerbread house. Their hands were sticky with icing and Samantha's cheek was striped with chocolate, but their gingerbread cottage was neat and tidy. It wasn't as large as the house Samantha had planned, and it didn't have a drawbridge, but there was a path of colored sugar wafers that looked like cobblestones leading up to the front door.

"You're clever in the kitchen, Miss Cornelia," Mrs. Hawkins said.

Cornelia blushed and pushed a silky curl out of her eyes. "Oh, it's nothing really," she answered. "I've always enjoyed cooking, Mrs. Hawkins."

"Well, it's a credit to you," Mrs. Hawkins declared solemnly. "Nowadays, it seems, many a lady wouldn't know batter from butter!"

"Did I hear someone say 'butter'?" Uncle Gard asked, coming into the kitchen. "Good grief, Mrs. Hawkins! I do hope you're not buttering up Cornelia. We wouldn't want her to slip away!"

Samantha groaned. "Uncle Gard, that's an awful joke."

"Is it?" Uncle Gard asked innocently. "Well, I suppose it's an awful *good* joke."

"Oh, Uncle Gard, please stop," Samantha said.

"Okay, Sam. But it's time to go if we want to find our Christmas tree. Hawkins has already harnessed the horses."

Samantha hurriedly wiped her hands on a towel. "I'll be ready before you can say 'Merry Christmas'!" she called, racing to get her mittens, hat, and coat.

Hawkins held the horses steady as Samantha and Uncle Gard climbed into the sleigh. Uncle Gard slapped the reins over the horses' backs, and the sleigh glided down the path to the street. For several minutes Samantha and her uncle rode in silence. They shared the red wool blanket and waved to passing neighbors. Then, almost to herself, Samantha said, "Tomorrow is Christmas."

"It's come pretty quickly, hasn't it, Sam?"

"No, I don't think so," Samantha replied. "I've been planning for months. And of course," she added with a mischievous smile, "it took a long time to get *your* present ready."

"Oh?" Uncle Gard asked, pretending not to be interested.

"Yes. It's the nicest present of all, and you'll never, never guess what it is," Samantha said.

"Of course I will!" Uncle Gard announced. "Let me try. Is it smaller than a breadbox?"

"Quite a bit, yes."

"Is it green?"

"Parts of it are," Samantha told him.

"Could I ride on it?"

"Not at all," Samantha giggled.

"Does it sing?"

"No."

"Can it do handsprings?"

Samantha laughed. "No! Guess some more."

"Is it something that closes up?"

"It could . . ." Samantha said cautiously.

"Could I wear it on my head in summer?"

"You'd look silly if you did!"

"Aha! I know what it is!" Uncle Gard declared.

"Tell me," Samantha said.

"It's a baby turtle, of course."

"A baby turtle?" Samantha gasped. "How do you figure that, Uncle Gard?"

"Because, Sam, everyone knows a baby turtle is smaller than a breadbox, cannot sing or do handsprings, is part green, can close up, cannot be ridden, and would look silly on my head in summer."

"Well, you're wrong," Samantha said. "It's not a baby turtle. It's something I made. And it's very beautiful. In fact, it is the most beautiful thing I've ever made for anyone."

"I'm sure I will love it, Sam," Uncle Gard said.

"I wonder what you'll give *me* for Christmas?" Samantha asked slyly.

"No, you don't!" Uncle Gard said. "Don't you try to trick me into telling you."

"Please give me some clues," Samantha begged.

"Okay, I'll give you three clues and no more. Clue number one: like a good schoolgirl, it uses *notes.*

Clue number two: unlike Samantha, it always *plays* alone. Clue number three: it's *bound* to please you."

Samantha was so puzzled by these clues that she sat deep in thought while the sleigh glided through the silent woods. When they reached the frozen river, Uncle Gard stopped the horses and tied the reins to a low willow branch. He lifted an ax from the back of the sleigh and caught Samantha's hand as she jumped down into the soft snow. Then they walked together, looking for just the right tree.

"This is it, Uncle Gard," Samantha said at last.

"You're right, Samantha. It's a real beauty."

Uncle Gard chopped away. The ax's loud whacks echoed through the stillness, and Samantha didn't talk as they dragged the tree back to the sleigh. On the way home, the horses' bells jingled brightly to the *clip-clop* rhythm of their hooves.

Exchanging Gifts

CHAPTER 18

I believe Mrs. Hawkins really outdid herself this year," Uncle Gard said as he pushed his chair back from the table. "Dinner was a feast!"

The aroma of plum pudding still hung in the air, and the red candles burned low in their polished holders. Samantha couldn't wait a moment longer. "Grandmary, now may we decorate the tree?" she asked.

"Of course," Grandmary replied cheerfully.

They gathered in the parlor and began to unpack the ornaments. Grandmary lifted a pair of little glass slippers out of the big oak chest. "These belong where they'll catch the light," she said. "I've watched them sparkle since I was six years old." She draped their golden cord over a long branch. Uncle Gard put a brass trumpet nearby. Cornelia placed the long-necked crystal swans near the top of the tree, where they seemed to float in the branches. And Samantha hung all of her blue silk angels right in the front, where Cornelia insisted they should be.

Soon it was time to attach the little white candles. Then slowly, one by one, Uncle Gard lit them. The effect was glorious. China rosebuds gleamed, crystal swans sparkled, and silk angels shone in the flickering light. Foil-wrapped sugarplums bobbed and twinkled, and miniature brass trumpets winked brightly. Grandmary's glass slippers seemed to dance.

They watched in silence, until Cornelia stepped over to the piano and began to play and sing:

"O Christmas tree, O Christmas tree,
How lovely are your branches."

Uncle Gard joined in, and Samantha and Grandmary sang, too. When the song was finished, Cornelia began another Christmas carol. They all sang and sang until the last candles on their beautiful tree burned low.

Later that night, while Samantha lay awake listening to street carolers in the distance, she thought again of the lovely Nutcracker doll. *Right now she's probably under some girl's Christmas tree, wrapped in pretty paper and waiting to be opened,* Samantha thought. She tried to think of something else, but it was no use. *If only I had even asked Grandmary for the doll, at least I'd have a chance of finding it under my tree tomorrow morning,* Samantha thought. *Now there's no chance at all.* She fell asleep to the sound of Christmas carols and dreamed of the beautiful doll dancing away from her, farther and farther away.

"Where is everybody?" Samantha asked on Christmas morning. She had hurried downstairs with her pink hatbox full of gifts to find that she was the only one awake. The grandfather clock in the parlor chimed seven o'clock.

Samantha looked around the parlor. The Christmas stockings at the mantel bulged with treats. A small mountain of presents already stood underneath the tree. "To Dear Samantha from Grandmary" was written on a box that wasn't nearly as big as the doll in Schofield's window. Samantha sighed and began to arrange her own presents under the tree.

She heard a rustling sound behind her. "Merry Christmas, Samantha," Cornelia said. She wore a forest green dress and carried a pile of presents.

"Merry Christmas," Samantha answered.

A moment later, Grandmary and Uncle Gard were in the parlor, too. "Merry Christmas!" Samantha called.

Grandmary sat down next to the tree. "I've asked Mrs. Hawkins to hold breakfast until eight, so we can exchange gifts right away. I know how you hate to wait, Samantha." She handed Samantha a package. "For you, my dear. Merry Christmas."

Inside was a sewing kit, a very grown-up one with forty different colored threads, a thick package of needles, and a cat-shaped pincushion. Samantha loved the way everything in the kit was arranged in its own special compartment.

"Oh, Grandmary, thank you," exclaimed Samantha. "Thank you so much." She gave her grandmother a warm hug. "Now I have a present for you," she said. She handed Grandmary her gift.

"It has a delightful fragrance," Grandmary said. "I can smell it right through the paper!"

"Can you guess what it is, Grandmary?"

"Not at all, dear. I'm quite perplexed so far."

Very slowly Grandmary took off the paper. When she found the heart-shaped sachet she said, "Samantha, you're a dear and clever girl. This is very lovely."

Next came a present from Uncle Gard to Samantha. "Here's your answer to those riddles, Sam," he said.

Samantha ripped off the wrapping paper and found a red leather book of Christmas carols. She turned the pages carefully, humming songs as she went. When she reached the end of the book, Samantha found a golden key. She wound it and a music box began to play her favorite song of all—"O Christmas Tree."

"Now I understand, Uncle Gard!" Samantha exclaimed. "You said my present would use notes and play alone because it's a music box. And it *is* bound to please me because it's a book of my favorite Christmas carols, too. Now I can listen to them all year round. Thank you, Uncle Gard. It's wonderful!"

Samantha was about to give Uncle Gard a small square box covered in blue tissue paper, but Cornelia handed her a large package instead.

"Go ahead, open yours first, Sam," Uncle Gard said with a wink.

Samantha had never seen anything wrapped so elegantly. She untied the silk ribbon and carefully rolled it up. "Cornelia, is this from New York?" asked Samantha.

"Open it and see."

Samantha smoothed away the silvery wrapping paper and slowly lifted the lid from the box. "Cornelia!" she gasped. "It's the Nutcracker doll! Oh, I've wanted this doll for the longest time. How did you ever know?"

"I didn't know, Samantha," Cornelia said. "Truly I didn't. It's only that *I* liked the doll so much, I thought perhaps you might, too."

"I do," Samantha said. She hugged the doll as if she'd never let it go. "I love her. I love her more than any other doll in the whole world. Thank you, Cornelia. Thank you so much!"

With the doll still in her arms, Samantha reached under the tree. Once again she picked up the small square box wrapped in blue tissue paper. But this time she turned to Cornelia and handed it to her. "Merry

Christmas, Cornelia," Samantha whispered.

"And Merry Christmas, Uncle Gard," Samantha said more loudly, handing him a larger package tied with a big pink bow.

Uncle Gard got his present unwrapped first. "By Jove, Sam!" he said when he opened the candy. "There must be a pound of chocolates here. You do spoil me!"

"Oh, Samantha, it's so very pretty!" Cornelia exclaimed when she saw the decorated box. "Why, look at all these tiny pictures! This must have taken you a long time to make."

"It did," Samantha said honestly. "That box took me longer than any other thing I've made. Ever!"

"I will keep my jewelry in it and treasure it always," Cornelia said.

Samantha caught Uncle Gard's happy wink. She thought he guessed that the box had been made for cuff links, but he seemed to understand why she'd given it to Cornelia.

Now Uncle Gard turned to Cornelia and said, "I think you need something special to keep in such a beautiful box, my dear." He handed her a tiny gift wrapped in dark red paper with a large gold bow on top. When Cornelia opened it, a diamond ring sparkled in the Christmas morning sunlight.

"Oh, Gard," she murmured softly.

But Samantha was so overjoyed she shouted, "It's an engagement ring! They're going to marry! Grandmary, isn't it wonderful?"

"Children, I'm so happy." Grandmary's voice was quivery, and she had to dab her eyes with her hankie.

"When is the wedding?" Samantha couldn't wait to find out.

"In the spring," the couple answered together.

"You *will* be my bridesmaid, won't you, Samantha?" Cornelia asked.

"Yes, I'd love to!" Samantha answered, and gave her a big hug. "Oh, Cornelia, this *has* been the best Christmas ever!"

INSIDE Samantha's World

In 1904, proper young ladies like Samantha wore elegant dresses covered with frilly aprons, high buttoned shoes, and long stockings held up with garters, even when they were playing. They couldn't climb trees in a pair of jeans, as girls do today. In fact, it really wasn't proper for young ladies to climb trees at all!

Well-to-do families like Samantha's lived in large, fancy houses that were decorated with fine furnishings. The elegance and comforts of proper life in 1904 were possible because there were many servants to do the work. A cook like Mrs. Hawkins spent nearly all day making meals for a family from scratch, since there were very few convenience foods like cake mix or canned soup. A maid like Elsa scrubbed the floors and cleaned the sooty gas lamps that lighted a proper home. A servant like Hawkins tended the garden and took care of the horses and carriage that people used instead of a car.

The lives of servants were not very comfortable or elegant. They worked long days for little money. Servants were expected to do their work without complaint and to keep their "proper" place—separate from the family they worked for. They ate separately and often lived in small rooms in the attic or above the carriage house. Servants were not supposed to visit with the parents or play with the children.

Even though a servant's life was a hard one, there

were plenty of people willing to do these jobs. Many of the people living in American cities were poor. They would do any kind of work just to help their families survive. If they weren't servants, they often worked in factories for long hours and little pay. Children like Nellie went to work to help their families earn money. Even though there were laws that said children should not work, some poor children disobeyed them so that they could earn money to help their families.

Young ladies like Samantha did not work. Drying dishes or making a bed was not considered a proper thing for them to do. In fact, Grandmary would not have expected Samantha to ever work, even as an adult.

But modern women like Cornelia believed that women should do much more than run elegant households. In 1904, more and more young women began going to college to become teachers and nurses. They wanted to help the people who lived in city slums make sure that poor children went to school instead of working.

In 1904, most children went to public schools, but wealthy children like Samantha often attended academies where students were either all girls or all boys. In addition to their regular schoolwork, girls at these schools had classes in *penmanship,* or handwriting, dancing, French, and drawing. They even learned how to walk, talk, sit, and bend gracefully, which were considered important lessons for young ladies.

Read more of SAMANTHA'S stories,

available from booksellers and at *americangirl.com*

Classics

Samantha's classic series, now in two volumes:

Volume 1:
Manners and Mischief
Making friends with a servant isn't proper for a young lady—but that won't stop Samantha!

Volume 2:
Lost and Found
Samantha finally finds her friend Nellie—living in an orphanage! She's determined to help Nellie escape.

Journey in Time

Travel back in time—and spend a day with Samantha!

The Lilac Tunnel

What is it really like to live in Samantha's world? What if you're a servant rather than a proper young lady? Find out by choosing your own path through this multiple-ending story.

Mysteries

More thrilling adventures with Samantha!

Clue in the Castle Tower
Samantha's visiting a grand English manor—haunted by a ghost!

The Cry of the Loon
A series of strange accidents at Piney Point has Samantha worried.

The Curse of Ravenscourt
Samantha has a new home—and it's putting everyone in danger!

The Stolen Sapphire
Samantha realizes that someone on her steamship is a jewel thief.

A Sneak Peek at

Lost and Found

A Samantha Classic

Volume 2

Samantha's adventures continue in the second volume of her classic stories.

Samantha and Grandmary rode through the streets of New York City until the horse-drawn cab stopped in front of Gard and Cornelia's tall, narrow brownstone house. Samantha had just hopped out onto the sidewalk when she heard voices shouting, "Samantha! Samantha!" She looked up. Agatha and Agnes were leaning out of a window high above her, waving wildly. Agnes looked exactly like Agatha. They were Aunt Cornelia's twin sisters. Now that Uncle Gard and Cornelia were married, Agnes and Agatha were Samantha's newest friends and favorite relatives.

"Hello!" Samantha called. She skipped and waved, already swept away by the twins' high spirits.

Agnes held up Jip, Aunt Cornelia's puppy, and waved his paw. Jip barked and wriggled with joy.

"We'll be right down!" Agatha yelled. Then she and Agnes and Jip disappeared from the window.

Cornelia smiled as she came down the front steps to Samantha and Grandmary. "Welcome!" she said. Just then the twins and Jip came flying out the door and down the steps. "Hurray! You're here!" they said as they hugged Samantha. Aunt Cornelia laughed.

"Come in, come in," she said. "As you can see, we're all very glad you're here."

The twins led Samantha into the dark, cool house. Uncle Gard was waiting just inside the doorway. He blinked at Samantha and said, "There you are, Sam! I've been looking for you all week long. I can't seem to find anything in this new house."

"Do you think you could help us find some lunch?" asked Aunt Cornelia.

"Certainly, certainly," said Uncle Gard, kissing the tip of her nose. "When it comes to finding food, I never have any trouble."

"Come on, Samantha!" said Agnes and Agatha. They pulled her into the dining room and made her sit between them. Then, both at once, they began showering her with questions. "Have you seen that terrible Eddie? How was your train ride? Do you want to go to the park after lunch? Do you want—"

"Girls!" Aunt Cornelia scolded gently as the maid began to pass the food. "You'll put Samantha in a spin with all your questions! There will be plenty of time for chatter later. I haven't even had a chance to ask Grandmary where she plans to shop today."

"I'll shop at O'Neill's, of course," Grandmary said.

"There's a fine new shop on Fifth Avenue that's closer than O'Neill's," said Uncle Gard. "What was the name of that store, Cornelia?"

Grandmary patted his arm and smiled. "Don't trouble yourself to remember, Gardner," she said. "I shall go to O'Neill's. I've shopped there for more than thirty years. I'm too old to change my ways now."

"O'Neill's is near Madison Square Park," said Aunt Cornelia slowly. "That area may be quite crowded today. There's a meeting in the park."

"I know," said Grandmary. "We passed it on our way from the station. Those suffragists were already blocking traffic." She shook her head. "In my opinion, ladies should not gather in public places. *Especially* not to carry on about this voting nonsense."

"Nonsense?" Aunt Cornelia asked. Her voice rose ever so slightly.

"Of course," said Grandmary. "Voting is not a lady's concern. It never has been. I see no reason to change things now. Those suffragists are making spectacles of themselves. They should stay at home where ladies belong."

Samantha saw Agnes and Agatha look at each other with raised eyebrows, then quickly look down into their soup bowls.

Aunt Cornelia opened her mouth to say something, then shut it again.

Samantha was bursting with curiosity. "But why—?" she began to ask.

"Well, well, well," interrupted Uncle Gard. "Well, well. The strangest thing happened to me as I was walking home from work the other day. A man came up to me and said, 'Do you know any girls who just turned ten years old?' And I said, 'Why, yes, in fact I do know one.' And he said, 'Would you give her this large box? There's something inside she might like.' So I brought the box home. It's out in the hall. Perhaps you'll open it, Sam, and show us what's inside."

Samantha forgot all about her questions. She and the twins ran from the table and opened the door. Jip was waiting right outside. He barked and jumped as the twins helped Samantha tear off the wrapping paper and open the box. Inside was a pram—the prettiest doll carriage Samantha had ever seen. It was deep red with shiny brass wheels. "Jiminy!" Samantha whispered. "It's beautiful." She ran to give Uncle Gard a big hug. "Thank you, Uncle Gard. Thank you very much!" She knew perfectly well the doll carriage was from Uncle Gard and no one else.

"Let's take it to Gramercy Park right now," suggested Agnes, who was as excited as Samantha.

"That *would* be fun." Samantha said eagerly. "May we go?"

"Certainly," said Uncle Gard.

"Can Jip come, too?" asked Agatha. "You know how he loves the park."

"No, I don't think that is a good idea," said Aunt Cornelia. "Remember what happened at Samantha's party when he ran away from you?"

"Oh, but nothing like that will happen *here*," said Agatha quickly. "The park has a fence all around it."

"Please, please, please?" begged Agnes.

Aunt Cornelia thought for a moment.

"We'll only be across the street in the park," wheedled Agatha.

"And you won't go any farther than that?" asked Aunt Cornelia.

"No!" the twins promised together.

"Will you keep Jip on his leash?"

"Yes!" shouted the girls.

"Promise?"

"Absolutely!" they cried.

"Well, all right," Cornelia finally agreed. "But—"

"Hurray!" the twins interrupted. Jip began yipping in excitement.

"Please be calm for just a minute," Aunt Cornelia said seriously. "I'm going to a meeting, but I'll be back at three-thirty. When I get back, we'll walk to the ice cream parlor to meet Grandmary. Don't forget."

"And don't forget to behave like young ladies," added Grandmary.

"And don't forget the rule about keeping Jip on the leash," repeated Aunt Cornelia.

"And don't forget to have a good time," said Uncle Gard, shaking his finger at them.

"We won't!" said the girls. And Jip barked to show that he agreed.

About the Author

SUSAN ADLER loved learning about what America was like in 1904 while she wrote about Samantha. Now she continues to learn about other times and places through her work in art conservation. Ms. Adler lives with her family on the East Coast.